Fine place for an ambush, Willie told himself as he turned the pinto in the direction of the shooting. Now other rifles had joined the fight. Willie howled furiously and slapped the pinto into a gallop. Man and rider flew across the rugged landscape.

A wiser man might have thought things out, made a plan. Only a fool rushed headlong into a fight. But then war had always been a fool's game. For three years Willie Delamer had ridden the forests and fields of Virginia relying on instinct and nerve for survival. It was the howling gray ghost of a cavalryman who now charged through a stand of junipers, firing twin pistols and scattering three cowboys as he raced along to a boulder-strewn hollow where Jesse Cobb fought desperately to hold on.

CLEAR FORK

G. Clifton Wisler

FAWCETT GOLD MEDAL • NEW YORK

A Fawcett Gold Medal Book
Published by Ballantine Books
Copyright © 1990 by G. Clifton Wisler

Library of Congress Catalog Card Number: 90-93045

ISBN 0-449-14655-3

Manufactured in the United States of America

First Edition: September 1990

for Barbara Puechner

CHAPTER 1

Texas in August was a torment. There wasn't a plant or an animal in that country without thorns or teeth. Everything seemed to tear at a man—or bite or sting! And the fiery yellow sun blazed overhead, baking the land and scorching any soul foolish enough to venture out onto the treeless plain.

Willie Delamer shrank beneath that relentless sun. Sweat streamed down his forehead and stung his eyes. His shirt was near soaked through, and the weary pinto pony beneath him stumbled onward.

"Easy, boy," Willie whispered hoarsely. "Not much farther."

No, the wide much-trodden sweep of the Western Cattle Trail to Dodge City was just a few miles back. Ahead, where muddy Clay Creek emptied itself into the Clear Fork of the Brazos, lay the cavalry post of Fort Griffin. Beyond that Ted Slocum's horse and cattle ranch straddled the river.

"Easy, boy," Willie said again as the horse shuddered. "Here, let's have ourselves a drink."

Willie nudged the exhausted animal toward the Brazos, then slid down from the saddle and splashed into the shallows. The pinto plunged into the cool water and whinnied its delight. Willie stepped out into the channel until the water lapped at his thighs. Then he sat down in the sandy bottom and ducked his face under the surface a moment.

1

"Lord, it brings you back to life," Willie called to the horse as he tossed his old gray hat to shore and shook the water out of his hair. After two days of riding the dry, desolate llano south of the Red River, staring at the elusive spotted mesas and reeling beneath the daunting sun, it felt incredibly good to be wet and cool. He cupped his hands and scooped up a portion of river water.

He paused a moment before drinking. Whoever had named that stretch the Clear Fork had either been blind or had a Texas cowboy's sense of humor. At its best the river tended toward muddy. Most days it was greenish brown and full of swirling sand. As to its taste, not even a Texan would have termed it sweet. The river crossed salt beds aplenty, and anyone taking a drink knew it.

Willie forced the salty liquid down his gullet. Water and salt were good for a man crossing the sunbaked inferno. In truth the bite of the water took him back to other, better times. For more than anything else the Clear Fork of the Brazos tasted like home.

"Home?" he whispered as he peeled off his shirt and rinsed the dust and sweat from the coarse cotton cloth. "Ain't known a home in ten years!"

It was an admission he'd never have allowed himself had human company been near. But as he pried his boots from his feet and stripped off trousers and drawers, he was taken back to a world he long thought lost to memory and recollection. He'd swum that stream before, as a tadpole of a boy with Trav Cobb, with his father and brothers after long days tending cattle, while hunting buffalo with old Yellow Shirt's Comanches at thirteen. Or was it fourteen? Did it really matter? Back then, sharing dangers and adventures had bred a rare understanding. Between men of honor like Big Bill Delamer and Yellow Shirt, there'd been little need for written treaties. Promises made and sealed with a handshake and the smoking of a pipe were honored by men of goodwill.

Those times were like the cold ashes of a campfire—only stories for sharing on winter nights by old-timers. The Comanches were gone now. Big Bill had fallen at Shiloh trying to take a hill that couldn't be taken. And Yellow Shirt was shot down by an emigrant farm boy who didn't know a peace chief from a prowling coyote.

Willie swam the river for half an hour. Then he stepped to the bank, set his clothes up in the lower limbs of a nearby willow, and returned to the shallows. Staring at the grizzled features reflected in the still water, Willie couldn't help sighing. Was it possible the reckless sandy-haired renegade who had left Texas ten years before could have turned into that weary-looking old man?

There were reasons for the wrinkles in his forehead, for the purple blotches on his chest, and the older, reddish scars left by bullets and sabers in Tennessee and Virginia. Those wounds had been his life. They spoke of the pain, of the hard fights, of the good friends left behind. They announced Willie Delamer a fierce fighter.

That's all in the past now, Willie thought. I buried that side of me in Colorado.

Yes, he'd fought his final battle there. He'd killed Mike Dunstan, that dark cloud that had swept through his life too often. And he'd left with his sister Mary and her boys the legacy he'd carried across battlefields and mountains—Big Bill's saber and the weathered blue banner under which he'd led his second son, William Delamer III, to Shiloh.

"I buried everything but my name," Willie whispered as he turned eastward, toward the Trident Ranch torn from his grasp by brother Sam. Yes, the past rested in a peaceful grave. Billy Starr, Wil Devlin, Jack Fletcher . . . all those stone-jawed killers had died. The road ahead lay open. Ahead loomed reunion with old friends—and peace. If there was such a thing.

He rose from the river and dragged himself up onto the rocky bank. The wind and sun were making short work of his clothes, and after drawing a clean pair of drawers from his saddlebags, he slipped them on and waited there for the other clothes to finish drying.

Downstream a pair of turkey buzzards turned slow circles overhead. Maybe they'd find a dead rabbit or a stranded fish. Maybe a stumble-footed cow would fall down a ravine. The

3

big birds seemed to haunt the llano, waiting for death to come. It arrived regularly.

As the wind whined through the willows, a voice seemed to haunt Willie's thoughts.

"Nothing is ever truly lost," the voice advised. "If a man loses something, goes back where he lost it, and looks carefully, he will find it."

Old Tatanka Yotanka, the Lakota medicine man, had said that a year ago.

"Even your heart?" Willie had asked. "Your soul?"

The old man had answered with a knowing smile, and Willie had started south. Tatanka Yotanka, after all, saw things in his dreams. He was a man of power. Wasn't he the same Sitting Bull the whites now said had painted the Little Big Horn with the blood of Custer's Seventh Cavalry?

"Old man, I pray you're right," Willie had said as he paced beside the river. He'd come to search out that peace, hadn't he? Sure, there'd been that diversion in Colorado, and a fight or two since. But nothing had dissuaded him from the notion that real peace waited nearby.

Wasn't it on the Brazos I lost it? Willie asked himself. It's there I have to look.

He sat beneath the willows and waited patiently for his clothes to dry. It was perhaps no more than a few minutes, but it seemed more like hours. A sudden urgency permeated his being, and he was eager to resume the journey. Once the last touch of dampness had left his trousers, he scrambled into them, threw on his shirt, and stepped into a pair of moccasins. The boots would be a long time drying still, and he wouldn't wait for them. Instead he tied them behind his saddle and mounted the pinto.

It was late afternoon when Willie approached the clutter of stone and picket buildings that made up Fort Griffin. He rode past with hardly a second glance. Nearby a small Indian village sprang up beside the river. For a second Willie thought the Comanches might have returned. Upon closer examination he identified the Indians as Tonkawas—likely cavalry scouts. One or two called to the man with the gray hat, and a boy raced alongside the pinto. Willie moved along after

4

nodding to the Tonkawas. There was a sort of kinship born to displaced people, he decided. Once, not so very long ago, the Tonkawas had a reservation downstream near old Fort Belknap. Then, in '59, the cavalry chased them and the other peaceful tribes north of the Red River. During the war the tribe had nearly been exterminated by its enemies, and the hundred or so survivors now huddled beside the fort.

Yes, I know what it's like to be hunted, Willie thought. And to lose a home, a family, everything!

In stark contrast to the sunbaked fort and its neighboring Tonkawa camp, the collection of clapboard sheds and grog houses known as Fort Griffin Town seemed downright beautiful. Piano music drifted through the steamy air, mixing with laughter and shouting to drown out disappointed mutters and painful wails. Scantily clad women with painted faces and hard, cold eyes sat outside rows of yellowing tents. Stunted children dragged buffalo hides from open-bed wagons or fetched pails of water to a bathhouse. A few soldiers strolled the dusty street or tried their luck at the gaming tents.

It was a sad place in spite of the lively music. Those shanty stores and flimsy grog houses had been built on profits made from buffalo hides and Comanche corpses. Yes, it was a town of blood and death. Back in Kansas, Texas cowboys had boasted of their exploits in that place. Some called it Sinville or Deviltown. Most knew it as the Flat.

"They say the Flat has itself a man for breakfast, lunch, and dinner," one drover had told Willie across the table of a Dodge City saloon. "I kilt one there myself."

Gazing at the faces of bitter buffalo hunters, forlorn soldiers, and wishful youngsters, Willie didn't doubt death lurked ever near. A man with nothing to lose doesn't risk much.

Willie rode past a dozen grog shops. He finally halted his horse outside a hovel on the east side of town. MARIA'S CANTINA was scrawled across an oak plank beside the open door. There was a wondrous rich aroma flowing from the place.

"Water your horse, mister?" a frail, sandy-haired child of fourteen or so asked, racing over as Willie dismounted.

"How much?" Willie said, examining the boy's patch-work pants and ragged shirt.

"Two bits," the youngster quickly answered. He gazed around as other urchins hurried up the street. "A dime? Please, mister, I ain't eat anything in two days."

"Here," Willie said, handing over the reins along with a quarter. "Water him first, though. See it's done, too, or I'll look you up."

"Yes, sir," the boy answered, offering up a poor excuse for a salute. "Trust me to do you a good job, General!"

A dozen others soon gathered. They offered to brush the pinto, polish Willie's boots, or fetch spirits. One even promised to arrange for company.

"You lookin' for somebody, mister?" one ragged boy asked. "I know 'em all. For a silver dollar I'd even set up the shot for you, say down at the bathhouse or over to Miss Myra's. Man'd be distracted."

"Get along," Willie urged, frowning sourly. "I didn't come here for trouble."

The disappointed faces merely pressed closer, and they only fled when Willie touched his fingers to the wooden grips of his twin Colt pistols.

Willie then ambled along to the cantina and stepped through the gap in the canvas wall that served as a door. Half-drunken men dressed in buckskins and buffalo hides sat on the floor nursing bottles. A pair of cavalrymen sat at a table and sipped shots of whiskey as they played cards. Three other tables were deserted. Willie sat at one on the far right side, facing the door, and waited for Maria.

He expected a lithe young Mexican girl to appear. Instead a two-hundred-forty-pound grandmother arrived with a platter of tamales and a heavy frown.

"Cost you a dollar for the table, señor," she announced. "For another dollar I feed you."

"Fair enough," Willie said, drawing a pair of silver pieces from his pocket and placing them on the table. "Got anything cool to drink?"

"Nothing cool in all of Texas," she barked. "I got some

beer ain't so bad. I keep it in the creek at night. Pretty warm now, though.''

"I'll try it,'' Willie told her.

"Fifty cents two glasses. Dollar for a pitcher.''

"Don't aim on drinking myself stupid,'' Willy said as he stacked two quarters beside the silver dollars.

"Why you come here then?'' Maria muttered as she set the platter in front of him, snatched up the money, and headed for the plank bar to fetch the beer.

Willie started on the tamales straight away. They were just bits of shredded beef and mashed beans stuffed inside corn tortillas, but Maria had seasoned them with green chiles and red peppers that awakened a man's senses. For days Willie had subsisted on a steady diet of jerked beef and tasteless tinned beans. Maria's tamales were a delight!

As for the beer, it was warm and stale. He found himself missing the salty taste of the Brazos.

"What else you need, señor?'' Maria asked after a bit. "More beer maybe? Whiskey? I got some local stuff the soldiers like. Deviltongue, they call it.''

"No, thanks,'' Willie replied. "Tell me, Maria, you know where Ted Slocum's place is?''

"Who?''

"Ted Slocum. Big, friendly sort of a man. Has a fair-sized ranch east of here along the Clear Fork.''

"What you want to go there for?'' she asked, frowning. "He bring nobody trouble. You leave him alone, señor.''

"I'm an old friend,'' Willie explained. "We fought together in the war.''

"You forget your war,'' Maria advised. "That a long time over now. Leave Señor Slocum to himself. You eat some more? Drink? You stay and do it. I don't look like no map, do I?''

"I know every place for a hundred miles around,'' the young horse tender Willie had hired for two bits called, stepping into the doorway and eyeing the tamales with ill-concealed hunger.

"Vamoose, Gilberto!'' Maria shouted, and the boy retreated.

7

Willie scooped the last of the tamales in his left hand, finished off the beer, and hurried to the door. Gilberto accepted the food and ate greedily as he led the way around the side of the cantina to where the pinto drank from a bucket.

"Tell me about the Slocum place," Willie urged.

"I been by there plenty," the boy explained. "Big ranch with many good cows and some horses. Twenty miles east, I guess, at Buffalo Hollow. That's why I know it. I go with the hunters sometimes."

"Don't you have family, Gilberto?"

"Just Gil," the boy said, frowning. "Lost Pa in the war. Ma, well, she sort of lost me down south a few years back. Since then I find my own way. You think Mr. Slocum might use a boy on his ranch?"

"Maybe," Willie said, avoiding the boy's hopeful gaze. "Guess I could ask him when I get out there."

"I could come along. I don't weigh much. Don't eat a lot. You got a good horse. He'd carry us both."

"No, I got a bad habit of finding trouble," Willie answered. "You'd be better off here in town."

"Better off?" Gil cried, staring at the bleak surroundings.

"Better off than dead," Willie muttered. "Best I get on now. Here," he added, tossing the boy a second quarter.

The youngster's face regained its hard scowl, and Willie mounted up. He rode east without glancing backward. He dared not.

Willie nudged the pinto into a light trot. His belly was full, and his life had rare direction. He could imagine Ted Slocum's surprise when . . .

The crack of a whip and a terrible scream startled Willie and unsettled his horse. Off to the right twenty feet or so a dozen youngsters fled for their lives. Cowboys tossed their hats and howled in laughter. A white-haired man in his mid-twenties tossed a rawhide whip to a similar-looking companion, and the whip cracked across the back of a smallish black boy. Again the boy screamed as the lash tore into his flesh.

"Toby!" Gil called as he raced along the dusty street past the pinto and leaped at the black boy's attacker. The white-haired man tossed the first boy aside and with a satisfied cry lashed Gil as well.

For a moment Willie busied himself steadying his horse. He wanted, needed to ride past. After all, a pair of broad-backed black men made a rush in to rescue the boys. A pistol shot sent them scurrying for safety, though.

"Mr. Fielder, please help us!" the black youngster appealed, wincing from the sting of the whip as he gazed at a stern-faced giant cradling a big-bore Sharps.

"Ain't nobody goin' to help you!" the lasher insisted. "Nobody!"

Nobody? Willie thought. The words haunted him. The tortured faces of the boys reminded him of others—in Richmond and Nashville and a hundred places besides. In the camps of Cheyenne and Sioux. In the Big Horn gold camps and along Purgatory River.

"I'd judge that's enough!" Willie suddenly yelled as the white-haired men stripped the black boy's shirt, revealing long gashes that flowed red with blood.

"Oh, the sport's just started," the man with the whip insisted as he tore the rags from Gil's shoulders. The second man drew out a knife and grabbed Gil's threadbare britches, but the boy managed to kick himself free.

"Cas, best collect him!" the whipper shouted.

Gil managed three steps before a cowboy threw out a leg and tripped the boy. The knife-wielding bully pounced and grasped the fearful youngster by his hair.

"Scalp him, Cas!" the whipper urged.

"Might just peel him raw," Cas replied.

"No, I think you'll let him go," Willie announced as he slid off his saddle and drew a pistol from his hip. "Hear?"

"Mister, I'd leave us be," the whipper suggested, throwing the black boy to the ground and turning abruptly. "You'd be new hereabouts. Don't know the lay of the land."

"I know you two got size and years on them," Willie argued. "Don't figure that entitles you to cut on 'em."

"Who'd you be?" Cas asked. "Look at that gray hat on your head! I can see a no-account saloon rat stickin' his nose in, but you got the look o' one taught better. Mister, you forget what you fought for?''

"I never forgot anything in my whole life," Willie barked. "Now you let those two go."

"Not likely," Cas replied, touching the blade to Gil's cheek so that blood flowed. Willie fired a single shot at the villain's foot, and Cas dropped the knife. Gil raced to Willie's side and hid behind the nervous pinto.

"Take my horse," Willie said, nodding toward the reins.

"Mister?"

"Do it," Willie ordered.

"You don't know what you're about, friend," the whipper said, grinning broadly. "Ever hear o' Rufus Jarrett? He's our pa. Rode with Terry's rangers till the Yanks kilt him. Me and Caswell here, we were too young for the war. Not anymore, though. You might say we's carryin' on for pa."

"Jerome's right," Cas agreed. "Yanks stole our ranch, the stock, caused Ma and our baby brothers and sisters to starve! All for these mud-faced apes! We done our bleedin', you see. Gives us the necessary credentials for educatin' these fellows."

Jerome kicked the black boy out into the street and raised the whip again. Willie lifted the nose of his pistol and fired, tearing the whip from its owner's hand.

"Lord, Cas, my hand!" Jerome sobbed, showing the bloody stumps that had been the middle and ring fingers. "Cas!"

Caswell reached for a nearby rifle, but Willie sent a warning shot in that direction.

"Mister!" Cas shouted furiously.

"You feel real lucky, you just go ahead and try me!" Willie cried with cold, dauntless eyes. "Well? How 'bout the rest of you brave cowboys? Anybody with an itch to die?"

"Cas?" Jerome yelled as he dropped to his knees, clutching his mutilated hand.

The black boy managed to scramble to his feet and seek the shelter of the hider's wagon. The cowboys darted off to nearby grog sheds.

"It's over now," Willie announced, holstering his pistol and taking the reins from Gil.

"Ain't nothin' over!" Jerome howled. "We'll be rememberin' this!"

"Do that!" Willie yelled, turning to Gil. "Best lose yourself for a time, son."

"Where?" the boy asked with dead eyes.

Willie stared at the whitish skin stretched tightly over Gil's ribs. Blood from the lashing trickled down the boy's sides.

"Come on," Willie said, offering a hand. "I'll get you clear o' town. From there you're on your own, though."

"Sure," Gil muttered. "Always have been."

CHAPTER 2

Willie Delamer carried little Gil only as far as the nearest ranch.

"Maybe they can use a horse handler," Willie suggested when he halted the pinto.

"Don't you worry yourself after me, General," the boy said as he jumped down. "I can always find somethin' for my hands to do."

Willie offered Gil a shirt and a pair of silver dollars, but the boy declined.

"Man can't get by on what people'll give him, you know," Gil explained. " 'Sides, might be womenfolk around. Once they take to countin' my ribs, I'm sure to land a job."

Willie managed a faint smile in parting. Then he slapped the pinto's rump and galloped eastward.

The Clear Fork of the Brazos is a restless stream, winding its way easterly in a number of broad bends. Normally Willie would have cut across country rather than follow the river, but with only the vaguest of directions, he dared not stray from the river's banks. There were bound to be a hundred places that might pass for Buffalo Hollow, after all.

The first ten miles beyond the Flat, Willie paid little attention to the range crews or ranch houses he passed. Once in a while cowboys would trail him a ways, but once they were satisfied he posed no threat, they returned to their labors.

Later, though, Willie approached the drovers slowly, waving with an empty hand to indicate friendship.

"I'm looking for Ted Slocum's place on the Clear Fork," Willie called to a pair of shaggy-haired teenagers not far from where the river made yet another of its endless bends. "I got far to go?"

"What'd you want at the Slocum place?" the elder of the cowboys asked. "You got business there?"

"I mean no harm, if that's what you're after," Willie assured them. "Ted rode with my company during the war. Up in Virginia."

"Saw the hat," the younger man said, studying Willie. "Not too healthy wearin' reb hats hereabouts. Not these days anyhow. Lot o' Yank soldiers ride this range. They shot a man or two back in '72."

"Ain't '72 now," Willie argued. "How far's Ted's place?"

"Continue along the river," the older cowboy answered. "Still six, seven miles, I'd judge. At the main trail crossin'. Buff'lo Holler, they call the spot."

"Thanks," Willie said, waving as he rode off.

He spotted the mustangs an hour short of dusk. He'd made a camp of sorts on a hillside above the river and was gnawing at a chunk of dried buffalo meat when the pinto stomped restlessly. Minutes later a spry brown stallion with a splash of white across his brow thundered through the shallows and screamed out a challenge.

"Well, boy?" Willie called as he sprang to his feet. "Do we give that demon a run?"

The pinto screamed its answer, and Willie tossed a blanket atop the weary animal, added saddle and bridle, then secured both. In another moment he was mounted and headed out in pursuit of the white-faced devil.

Actually old white face wasn't alone. He led a harem of twenty-five mares and a fair assortment of colts. Those animals would have been a middling cash crop for most men, as range ponies made good workhorses for Texas cowboys. Willie had devoted a fair portion of his life to roping and breaking horses, but he didn't chase the ivory-nosed horse to make a fortune. No, he was merely answering a challenge.

13

The thirty or forty horses trailing the white-faced stallion raised a dust cloud that could be seen for five miles or more. Willie soon tired of choking on dirt and swung south from the river. The pinto snorted and panted as Willie urged extra effort. And before long Willie thundered past the harem and closed in on the stallion.

Willie couldn't help recalling the old days, hunting with the Comanches, racing ponies with Red Wolf, upholding the honor of the Second Texas at Corinth by trouncing an army of boastful Alabamans. He could feel the pinto's steamy breath, and as he bent lower, droplets of sweat flew off the lathered horse's neck and stung Willie's eyes. The white face was close now, and Willie drew out a rope. The fingers of his right hand made a loop in the rope, and he raised it high. The pinto brushed the side of the mustang, and Willie swung the loop over its head and held tight.

"Lord, we got him!" Willie whooped as the noose tightened, and the frantic mustang fought to escape. Willie knew his business, though. The rope held fast, and Willie drew in the slack a foot at a time.

"You met your match this time, white face," Willie boasted as he stared at the beaten horse. "You'd make a fair war pony. Or sire as fine a string of cow ponies as Texas ever knew."

The mustang dipped its head and struggled to break free. It was wasted effort, though. Suddenly Willie reached into his pocket and drew out a knife. With a sigh he pulled the rope close and slashed the knot, freeing the captured horse.

"Well, white face?" Willie called. "Ride!"

The mustang paused but a second. The rope now fell past one shoulder and lay on the ground. Screaming with fury, the mustang reared high into the air and turned away. Moments later the master was leading his harem back across the Clear Fork and north into the far hills.

"Guess you think I'm a fool, eh, boy?" Willie asked as he turned the pinto back toward the camp. "Brother Sam sure would. Others too. Papa would've understood, though. And Yellow Shirt. You can't put a bridle to the wind, after all. Some critters were meant to be free."

Willie was still laughing about the wild ride when he reached the camp. After unsaddling the pinto and leaving it to graze beside the river, he made a soft bed amid the long grasses and spread out his blankets there. Water bubbled out of a nearby spring, and Willie filled his canteens. Finally he kicked off his moccasins, shed his trousers, and unbuttoned his shirt. Only now did he feel a twinge in his side.

"Open her up again, did I?" he asked, staring at fingers painted red with blood. It hadn't been quite three weeks since Mary had carved a bullet from his hide.

"You shouldn't ride so soon," she'd warned. And as always, Willie had paid no heed. Well, it was only seeping a bit. Just natural. And there wasn't much pain. All in all he was faring awfully well for a dead man.

"Yeah," Willie muttered as he lay down in his blankets. He ought to be dead a dozen times over. The Yanks nigh killed him at Shiloh. The Sioux close to got him in the Big Horns. There was that other war on the Cimarron, the trouble on the Sweetwater, in South Pass, so many places. But he'd survived it all.

At least the flesh had. As to the soul . . .

Willie closed his eyes a moment and recalled the little amber-haired boy who had ridden at his father's side along the Brazos. Were there ever eyes so wide, a heart so eager to taste every challenge life might provide? Why was it all that had to change? What nightmare had taken him so far from the people and places he loved?

It was the war, of course. To begin with anyway. Bullets had struck down his father, and cholera had taken his mother. What had begun as a glorious adventure had become a ghastly nightmare. War had painted everything dark and ugly. It had left only a shadow of the old Willie Delamer—a shadow walking a world haunted by specters.

He stared downstream toward a distant pinprick of light. That would be a cattle camp. He listened intently, hoping to pick up the notes of a guitar or perhaps a song shared with the prowling stock. The wind was sweeping down from the Rockies, though, from the northwest, and only a monotonous whine blended with the chorus of crickets and tree frogs.

15

Willie closed his eyes and hoped sleep might capture him. He prayed for the soothing numbness that night sometimes brought. In the end he stared at the moon drifting in and out of a layer of clouds and recalled how on a night like this he'd first climbed the medicine cliffs above the Brazos with old Yellow Shirt. There, among the burial scaffolds of the ancients, Willie had first felt the touch of the great mystery, what the Sioux called Wakan Tanka.

Willie had stood tall there. He'd cut the leathery flesh of his chest so that blood ran down his naked thighs and dripped onto his feet. The faint white scars remained even now.

There was truth then, he told himself. Understanding. A man knew who he was, what he was.

That wasn't everything, Willie supposed, but it was enough.

"Where are you now, old friends?" Willie whispered to the whining wind. "Yellow Shirt? Red Wolf? Papa?"

They were on the other side, and the comfort their words, their wisdom, and their touch would have brought was forever denied him. But there was one friend left, one man who knew him from the old days, who'd shared the hard fights and the bitter memories. Most of them anyway. Travis Cobb. What was it Ted Slocum had said in Kansas? Trav was running cattle on the Clear Fork, too, now.

"Major, why don't you come along, join us?" Ted had suggested. And later Trav had written of it himself, passing the letter through his brother Lester, a Kansas lawman.

So now I've come, Willie thought. He was almost home. Suddenly that notion drove icy splinters of fear through his insides. Home? It was a word more frightening than an army of Sioux!

CHAPTER 3

Willie'd never been one to sleep much past dawn, and the faint golden glow on the eastern horizon was enough to stir him to life. He yawned away his weariness, took a glance at the grazing pinto down by the river, and threw off his blanket. The August heat was already making itself felt, and he wiped sweat from his forehead. Then he tugged on his trousers and stepped into his now dry boots.

"Be a fine day," he mumbled as he pulled a pair of stale biscuits and some dried beef from his saddlebags. "Too fine to waste abed." That was his father's favorite proverb. And a rare truth of sorts. In Texas a man didn't dare waste the cool morning hours. By midday the heat would melt anything that moved.

Willie crunched down on his breakfast and observed the rising sun. There wasn't a cloud in the sky, and the landscape appeared fresh—new. A man might imagine himself the only one alive there. Oh, sure, a chaparral poked its beak at a rattler, and a family of bobwhites rustled about in a thicket. But they kept to themselves, and Willie was content to do likewise. There was a peace that came with solitude. It was never altogether unwelcome.

After disposing of the last of the beef, Willie tossed the final crumb of biscuit in his mouth and set about saddling the pinto. The horse stirred anxiously, and Willie patted its

17

nose to calm the animal. Willie himself was no less excited. It couldn't be much farther to Buffalo Hollow now—to Ted Slocum and beyond there to the Cobb ranch.

Once Willie assured himself the saddle was secure, he rolled up his belongings in the blankets and tied them behind his saddle. Lastly he slipped into his shirt, placed the weathered Confederate cavalry hat on his forehead, and buckled on his pistol belt. It was time to resume his journey.

Again he headed eastward. For a time he snaked his way across the broken plain alone, the solitary trace of life on a bleak landscape. Then a red-tailed hawk rose out of a grove of live oaks. The hawk soared high against the pale blue Texas sky, then dove like an arrow upon an unsuspecting rabbit.

Yes, old friend, Willie silently told the hawk, I've been you. Content to sail along above it all—until it was time to pounce.

"No more!" Willie shouted. His words echoed across the empty land, taunting him. The hawk screamed as it flew past overhead.

"Better a hawk than a rabbit," Red Wolf had once observed. Willie wasn't so certain. For the rabbit the pain was over quickly. It lingered for the hawk.

As Willie urged his horse along through dry creek beds and crumbling ravines, he began to spot signs of life. Clusters of longhorn cattle gathered at the river to satisfy their thirst. The larger, bulkier shapes of grazing buffalo appeared as well.

"It's all over for you most places up north," Willie called to the woolly giants. "Time to sing a death chant. You won't last long on the Clear Fork."

The words rang true. Only a mile away the cumbersome wagons of hiders marked the site of a kill. A small army of misfits, mostly half-grown boys, cut hides from forty slain buffalo. The bare shoulders and stick-thin legs of the boys were spattered with blood and grit. Each face that glanced his way seemed to stare with cold desperation. They all resembled little Gil. And their eyes mirrored his own.

"Seen any buffs upriver, mister?" a burly hunter called

from beside a small campfire. "We only cut ourselves off a quarter of this herd. Others'd be out that way, I'm guessin'."

"Didn't see 'em," Willie lied. "Could be there just the same."

"Got some coffee brewin'," the hunter shouted. "Mashed the beans myself just this mornin'. Share a cup with us, will you?"

Two other hunters joined the first. There was something distant, forlorn about their faces. The pinto sniffed the air and stomped fitfully. The wind carried an odor of blood and death.

Willie smelled only the coffee, and he readily joined the hunters. No names were exchanged, for men with pasts to boast of rarely took to the hunting grounds. Nor rode alone. Instead they spoke of buffalo and Comanches and days coming to an end.

"Saw that Sharps tied back o' yer saddle, friend," the first hunter mentioned at last. "I'd say you got the look of a hunter yerself. Care to join the outfit? We made ourselves a thousand dollars each last season, even after payin' the cutters."

"That's right," the others echoed.

"Fair profit, especially now the Comanches leave us be," the first man added. "Takes a keen eye, but I'd judge you have one. Well?"

"I'm weary of killing things," Willie confessed. "And I've got a place to go."

"Then you're the lucky one," the second hunter declared. "Not many hereabouts can boast as much. Good luck to you."

"Ever hear of a place called Buffalo Hollow?" Willie asked as he rose to leave.

"Know a hundred of 'em," the third man answered. "The one you'd be after's not two, three miles east. Good crossin' o' the river there. Buffs used to cross at the place till some Texan built himself a house and took to waterin' longhorns there."

"It'd be the spot I'm looking for," Willie told them. "Luck to you."

"To you, too, soldier," the first hunter called. "And if it don't pan out, we'll be around."

The others shared a chuckle. Willie found little humor to the matter, though. He knew their world, with its ocean of blood and quick, heartless death. He climbed atop the pinto and slapped it into a gallop. His solitary desire was to leave the place far behind.

The hunters weren't the last men Willie came upon that morning. Just a mile and a half ahead, not far from where he expected to spot Ted Slocum's ranch, a group of horsemen surrounded a horse-drawn buggy.

Willie laughed at the sight. The oilskin cover and polished brass hubs were out of place. He might have ridden on except he noticed the dusty, weathered appearance of the accompanying horses. Had the buggy perhaps fallen upon bad company?

Willie eased a pistol out of its holster and laid it on his right knee. He then edged closer.

"We got company, Mr. Fairchild," a sandy-haired cowboy announced, and a smallish, round-shouldered man dressed in a banker's suit emerged from his four unkempt companions. His dark, thinning hair was tinged with gray, and there was something cultured and polished about him that was as out of place as his buggy.

"Good afternoon, sir." Fairchild spoke with a heavy English accent. "Is there some way that I might serve you?"

"I thought maybe it was you needed some help," Willie confessed, tapping the drawn pistol against his hip.

"Oh," Fairchild said, gazing at the others with a broad grin. "One has to make do with what help he can find in Texas. They know the country, though."

"Do they?" Willie asked, taking note of the youthful faces. "You boys ever hear of Buffalo Hollow?"

"Just ahead o' you," one explained. "Over yon hill."

"Then I'd judge this ground here to be part of the Slocum place," Willie added sourly.

"No fence posts," the sandy-haired cowboy explained. "Hard to tell where one man's land starts and another's stops.

Anyway, Mr. Fairchild just wanted to have a look at the river crossin's.''

"Oh?" Willie asked.

"Just having a look around the countryside really," Fairchild said nervously. "I might choose to settle nearby."

"Land here's mostly taken already," Willie mentioned.

"Well, things get bought and sold here like anywhere else," the sandy-haired fellow pointed out. "Mr. Fairchild's got a habit for gettin' his way, you know."

"I believe that's quite enough, Deaton!" Fairchild scolded. "Mister . . . what did you say your name was?"

"I didn't," Willie replied. "Folks call me Wil."

"Mr. Wil, I'm certain you will understand that I mustn't linger in this sun," Fairchild said, stepping toward the buggy. "We've nothing to match it in Sussex, and it's scorched me proper, I fear. Deaton, you others, it's time we were off."

"Yes, sir," Deaton answered, waving the others toward their horses. "Ain't likely we'll see you again, Gray Hat. Might be best that way."

"Might be," Willie agreed as he returned Deaton's hard stare. The buggy soon bounced on toward the river, and Willie watched its escorting riders cautiously screen its passage.

Just good sense to take precautions, Willie told himself as Fairchild's little company became a distant swirl of dust. Likely the Englishman was out making a survey for a railroad. That was a bitter notion, railroads crossing the wild unbridled country. Yes, progress came even to the Brazos. Sighing, Willie turned the Pinto eastward and hurried along toward Buffalo Hollow.

He never actually got there. Just over the next hill he was met by a pair of young cowboys. The Bar TS brand on their horses marked them as Slocum hands. Their suspicious eyes betrayed their alarm.

"Hold up there, mister," the first boy said. Tall and thin, with curly walnut hair and clear blue eyes, he appeared older by perhaps a year. The second was even slimmer, but his fair hair and befreckled face made him seem somehow small.

Willie judged them to be fourteen or fifteen. He halted and waited for the wary pair to join him.

"Where might you be goin'?" the younger boy challenged.

"Not too friendly a way to meet a visitor," Willie remarked.

"Got lots o' visitors here lately," the older boy countered. "Yanks, most o' them, out to collect some fool tax or try to cheat us out o' stock or land."

"I look like a Yank?" Willie asked, pushing back the brim of his hat.

"Had a few gray hats through, too," the yellow-haired youngster explained. "Renegades mostly."

"Not the kind you'd invite home to supper, eh?" Willie asked.

"It's not always easy to tell a man's true colors," the younger boy replied.

"No," Willie agreed. "It's easier to spot a man by his family. You two, for instance, got a lot of Slocum to you. Noses in particular. The eyes must come from your mama. Ted's got those hard little walnuts that can stare you right down to your socks."

"Yeah?" the elder asked, backing his horse nervously. "What'd Pa be to you?"

"An old friend," Willie said, swallowing a sudden surge of emotion. "I'm doing my best to recollect names. Years. They all seem to run together. Gus and Elyssia'd be older. Am I right?" The boys reluctantly nodded. "Then you'd be Lamar," Willie said, pointing to the elder. "And your brother'd be called . . . Lewis, I think."

"You know a lot," Lamar observed as he ran his hand alongside the stock of a Winchester housed in its saddle scabbard.

"Comes with years," Willie explained. "And wrinkles. Ted used to talk about you two in particular. Especially Lewis. He never even saw you till after we came back from Virginia. Lamar, he'd pass the cold Petersburg nights recalling how he'd rocked you in his arms and listened to you babbling. And there were your mama's letters, all full of this

22

and that, the time you took your first steps or the day fever near took you the winter of '63.''

"How's he know that?" Lewis asked his brother.

"I didn't have many letters my own self," Willie told them. "Papa fell at Shiloh, and a fever carried Mama away. I didn't even know about her till I got home. There was a girl wrote for a time, but then that stopped, too. Your ma's letters were so full of love and family! Ted shared 'em. I believe it kept us alive."

"How?"

"Oh, she'd describe how the sun looked coming up over the river, or she'd write about the hailstones that came howling out of a March sky. Mostly it was the talk about you boys, and your brother and sister. The prayers you spoke for your papa's return. Those words warmed us through many a hard winter's night."

"You knew Pa in the war then?" Lewis asked with confused eyes.

"He ever tell you how he got that nick in his ear?" Willie asked. "We crawled out between the lines to swap tobacco with some Yank pickets for coffee to keep the men warm. My toes were close to frozen, and I don't think Ted was any better off. We made our trade just fine. Then this fool of a bluecoat colonel comes riding out, hollering about an attack and shooting off his pistol. One ball notched Ted's ear, and another one holed our coffee tin. Well, a soldier'll abide a lot of things, but he won't stand for his colonel fouling the tobacco trade."

"The Yanks shot their own colonel," Lamar added, laughing. "Right in the britches! I heard that tale a hundred times. And I figure there's just one man in creation'd spin it as well as Pa. He'd be dead by most accounts."

"Think so myself at times," Willie said, sighing. "Don't you see it in my eyes?"

"I do," Lewis admitted. "Makes a man jumpy, lookin' into them eyes."

"Unsettles him some to spy 'em in a looking glass," Willie added.

"Pa never talks much about the war nowadays," Lamar

23

said, relaxing his grip on his rifle. "Never about the fightin'."

"It's not the kind of memory to ease your sleep, boys," Willie told them.

"No, I expect not," Lamar agreed. "Meanwhile, you said somethin' about comin' home to supper. Care to give her a try?"

"Been a week and a half surviving on cold biscuits and dried beef. Some buffalo once, and tamales at Maria's Cantina in Fort Griffin Town yesterday."

"Then I'll bet some baked chicken'd set just right," Lewis boasted. "We'd welcome you to the table."

"Truth is," Lamar added, "we'd be more'n just everyday proud to escort you to the house, Major Delamer."

"Yes, sir, we would," Lewis agreed.

"Then lead on, boys," Willie urged. "I've a yen for some company."

CHAPTER 4

Willie followed the Slocum boys through the rolling hills a mile or so before arriving at the ranch. There was a long plank house up front, surrounded by two barns and a maze of cow pens and horse corrals. Between the barns stood a picket structure Willie judged to be a bunkhouse. Near one of the barns chickens pecked at feed. Hogs were penned up as well. All in all it was a fine, prosperous place.

"Pa?" Lewis called, riding ahead to where a cluster of men sat atop the rail of a work corral. "Pa?"

A tall, dark-haired man climbed down and greeted the boy.

"Lew, you finish collectin' them strays so soon?" the man asked.

"No, Pa," Lewis answered. "We come across somebody."

Ted Slocum turned slowly to where Lamar and Willie sat atop their horses. The rancher stared a moment, then approached slowly.

"Good Lord, it can't be," Slocum said, scratching his chin. "Major? Is it you?"

"Don't know any other fool who'd confess to it," Willie replied, tipping his hat. "Been a while, Ted."

"Kansas, three, four years back. Took you that long to find the Clear Fork, did it?"

"Been a ways in the meantime," Willie admitted. "Covered some ground."

"Trav's had letters from Les," Slocum said, motioning Willie to dismount. "And from Ellie. Last they heard you was up in the Rockies."

"Was," Willie admitted as he climbed down off the pinto. "But winter's hard up high."

"Hard everywhere," Slocum noted. "There'll be time to catch up later, though. Elvira's sure to have somethin' put by for supper. Long as we got these boys in off the range, might as well sit down to the table. You'll take a plate with us, won't you?"

"He's been chewin' cold beef and biscuits for days," Lamar declared. "Likely he'd kill for some o' Ma's chicken."

"I'm close to that hungry myself," Lewis said, grinning. "Give me your horse, Major. I'll see him tended."

"Come on, Major," Slocum said, stepping over and ushering Willie toward the house. "I want you to meet the rest of the family."

Willie nodded, then followed his old comrade toward the front porch. They stepped inside together, and soon thereafter Willie was met by the rest of the Slocums.

"Elvira, children, this here's Major Willie Delamer, late o' the Army o' Northern Virginia," Slocum announced. "And a few other fights before and since, accordin' to others."

"A few," Willie confessed as he offered a hand in greeting the graceful, amber-haired Elvira. She disdained the hand and instead wrapped both arms around Willie's waist and near squeezed him flat.

"Should've warned you, Major," Lewis said, laughing. "Ma's a hugger."

"She's a right to where some're concerned," Elvira argued. "I never got a proper chance to thank you for seein' my Ted through the war, Major. Nor for gettin' that first cattle drive to Kansas organized, either."

"Ma'am, it's me owes Ted," Willie insisted. "I was a young fool with more braid'n sense most o' the time. Steady soldiers like Ted, well, they were what got us all through."

26

"Not by most accounts," she countered.

"Well, Texans have a way o' stretchin' truths, I suppose," Willie said, grinning as she released her hold. "And you'd sure do me an honor by calling me Willie. I haven't been a soldier in more'n ten years now."

"I can manage Willie if you can try Elvira," she told him. "Now, I suppose you'd best meet the others."

Elyssia Slocum was the eighteen-year-old image of her mother. Her fair skin and yellow hair graced a gentle face, and her bright intelligent eyes seemed to notice everything at once.

"I'm pleased to meet you, Willie," she said without flinching. "Pa's said so much about you."

"This can't be the little girl you left behind in '62," Willie told Slocum. "I'll bet she's got every boy in ten counties chasing her."

"Just a couple of Cobbs," Lamar joked. "Especially Bobby. Bet they're married 'fore Christmas."

Elyssia fumed, and her father scowled. "Don't go makin' fun o' your sister, Lamar," Slocum warned. "She's sure to have her revenge ready."

"Yes, sir," Lamar answered, retreating.

"Come here, little ones," Slocum then called, and a shy pair of boys with nutmeg hair emerged from behind their mother.

"The bigger one's Hood," Lewis explained. "Named for your general."

"Littler one's called Hill," Elvira added. "After my papa."

"Glad to meet you both," Willie said, gripping their small hands. Hood might have been nine, and Hill was a couple of years younger. They hurried over beside their father, and Slocum wrapped a big arm around each.

"There was an older boy," Willie began, nervously glancing around the room. "Gus. Nothing's happened to him, I pray."

"Gone to market in Weatherford," Slocum explained. "Lord, he's gotten taller'n me, Major. All filled out and straight as an arrow. Fine man he's makin'."

"You've had good fortune," Willie observed. "It's a family to be proud of."

"Thank you, Willie," Elvira replied.

"They're a comfort," Slocum confessed. "And a torment sometimes as well."

"That's how it is with families, I suppose," Willie said, grinning as Hood and Hill hid behind their father and sneaked occasional peeks at their houseguest.

"Some more'n others, I guess," Elyssia muttered, turning away.

"Daughter!" Elvira barked.

"It's only the truth," the girl answered. "Everybody knows he's Sam Delamer's brother. Sure, Major Willie Delamer, a fine man and a good soldier! He's still a Delamer, though. It was Delamers chased the Cobbs off their own land, wasn't it? And look at Sam now. He's bought every inch of land along the river for fifty miles, and he'll turn to us next. I've heard him boast he'll own ten counties before he's forty. Jess Cobb says—"

"Hush!" Elvira ordered.

"No, let her talk," Willie urged. "I haven't heard more than a whisper about Sam in years. I doubt there's anything she could say that would much surprise me. After all, I'm the one Sam paid men to shoot bullets at."

"Pa?" Lewis gasped.

"I'm sorry," Elyssia said, paling. "I didn't know."

"That's why a sensible person holds her tongue in check," Elvira scolded. "Ted and I know what it cost you to ride to war, Willie. And what a bitter disappointment it was to come home. Will you see your brother now? Settle accounts?"

"That would mean somebody dying," Willie muttered. "I didn't come south to bury anybody."

"Why did you come?" Lamar asked.

"To see old friends," Willie answered. "And to find something I lost. It's hereabouts, I'm thinking. Or nowhere at all."

"And Sam?" Slocum asked.

"Needn't know I'm within a thousand miles," Willie said,

28

sighing. "I'd like to see my brother Jamie, maybe visit Mama and Papa, but—"

"Your folks're still on that hill by the river," Slocum interrupted. "Not hard, ridin' out there by night and stayin' unseen. As to James, you'd find him changed. He's a boy no longer. Read law for a time, served as a judge, and now he's down in Austin."

"Doing what?" Willie asked.

"He's a state senator," Elyssia answered. "Bought and paid for with Delamer money."

Willie frowned and rubbed his hands against his hips. Slocum only shook his head and suggested everyone head for the dining room.

"Wait till you taste some o' Ma's cookin', Major," Lewis said, hoping to brighten the mood. "What will we have anyway?"

"Roast chicken and peach pie," Elvira called. "Just as soon as certain menfolk I know scrub themselves proper. I won't have any horse scent at table."

"Horses!" Lewis cried. "I forgot all about 'em!"

The fourteen-year-old turned and hurried back toward the door.

"Best help him, Lamar," Slocum advised, and Lamar stumbled along as well. "Elvira, you best give it a few minutes. Seems our boys've neglected their chores."

"As usual," Elyssia said, laughing. "Brothers!"

"Must be a vexation to have so many," Willie told her.

"I read Job to learn patience," she replied. "But then one brother can be a trial, too, can't it?"

"Yes, it can," Willie confessed.

"That's enough, Elyssia," her father pronounced. "It's not Sam Delamer I've invited to table. I hesitate to call you to accounts for the shortcomings of your brothers."

"Yes, Pa," she said, nodding. "I'm sorry, Willie. I never considered that side of it. It's just that Bobby and his brother Jess hold a grudge against your family. It's hard to forget."

"Or to forgive," Willie acknowledged. "But like your papa said, Elyssia, I'm not Sam. If I'm around for long, you'll see that for yourself."

29

Elyssia gave a slight nod. Then Willie followed Slocum and the younger boys down a corridor to a small room containing a washtub and two small basins.

"Hood, that soap's not there to admire," Slocum said as the boys dipped their faces in the water. "Put it to work."

"Yes, Pa," Hood answered.

"You too, Hilly," Slocum urged.

"Yes, Pa," the smaller boy agreed.

Willie took his turn when the little ones had finished. It wasn't possible for a basin of water and a sliver of soap to scrub away a day's accumulated dust and sweat, but he did his best to make himself presentable.

"Later you'd likely care to have a turn at a tub, Major," Slocum declared. "I'll see water's heated."

"Later?" Willie asked.

"You surely didn't come such a great ways to hurry on off again," Slocum said, shooing Hood and Hill out the door. "Now look. I got more cows'n I know what to do with, and acreage I never see in a month. I set Trav up just east o' here, and I can do the same for you. Ain't your pa's place naturally, but it'd be on the Brazos, close enough, to my way o' thinkin'."

"Thanks, Ted, but I'm not sure I could trust myself to stay so close and . . ."

"Not have a talk with your brother?"

"I fear it'd come to more than words."

"Well, you *will* stay with us a bit. That's decided."

"Is it?"

"Try and ride off, Major. You'll have another war on your hands. The boys'll want a tale or two o' the Rockies, and I could use a firm hand with a pair o' cantankerous ponies I got myself saddled with."

"I'll give them a try," Willie promised. "After all, I intend to see Trav."

"And there's somethin' you were lookin' for."

"Yes, there's that," Willie agreed.

"As for now, we'd better get along to the table. Lamar and Lewis'll be a time yet. Elvira won't have much patience if we happen along late, too."

"Never smart to anger the cook," Willie declared.

"That's a wise man speakin'," Slocum said, laughing as he led the way from the small room. "And besides, you look to need some fattenin' up."

"I could eat something."

"Elvira's sure to have a fit if you don't clean a plate or two. She's partial proud o' her stove work."

Willie expected it was true. Elvira seemed to have plenty to be proud of.

Ted Slocum conducted Willie to the dining room and motioned toward a chair at the foot of the table. Elvira and Elyssia occupied the right side. Hood and Hill sat on the left. The two places on either side of Willie awaited Lewis and Lamar.

"In this house we never wait supper on wayward boys," Elvira announced. She then said a short prayer and began placing chicken onto plates. Willie accepted his, then added a pair of fluffy biscuits. In no time he was enjoying the wondrous meal.

Lamar and Lewis appeared ten minutes or so later. They underwent a brief inspection by their mother, then attacked their food. Willie couldn't help smiling. It was a wonder how much food a boy could devour.

Elyssia was less kind. "Piglets," she muttered.

There was considerable other conversation at the table that night, but Willie declined to participate. Mostly the Slocums spoke of family matters, of cattle prices, or of Gus's journey to Weatherford. Willie busied himself eating.

"Can I dish you up another helping?" Slocum finally asked.

"I've eaten a fair share," Willie reported. "And there's that peach pie to consider."

"I'll bring it out directly," Elvira declared. "Elyssia, won't you clear away the table, please."

"I could use some help," she pointed out, and Lamar begrudgingly accepted the job. As they carried off plates, their mother appeared with a pie tin. She cut steaming wedges of pie and gently laid them on small plates.

"Major's a wise man," Lewis said as he passed a piece

of pie into Willie's waiting hands. "Nobody bakes a peach pie like Ma does."

"I wouldn't dispute it," Willie said as he sampled the pie. "It's been a long time since I tasted the like, ma'am. Now I know why Ted hung on at Petersburg. He couldn't abide the notion of missing your pies."

Elvira blushed slightly, and Slocum laughed.

When supper finally reached its conclusion, Elvira dismissed all of her brood save Lewis.

"Your turn with the dishes, young man," she announced.

Lewis scowled, but a nod from his father silenced any objections. The boy trudged toward the kitchen while Elyssia began clearing the pie plates.

"If you wouldn't mind, I'll give the boy a hand," Willie offered.

"You're company," Elvira argued.

"It'd be a favor," Willie insisted. "I'll leave Lewis enough to do. Just dry and visit a bit."

"That's another matter," Slocum declared. "Welcome to it."

Willie joined young Lewis in the kitchen. Willie couldn't help pausing a moment to admire the place. Ted Slocum had installed a pump alongside a pair of tin tubs—one for washing and one for rinsing. Lewis was already at work pouring hot water from a kettle into the wash pan.

"I figured you could use a hand," Willie said as he grabbed a drying cloth. "Don't suppose you'll chase me off."

"No, sir," Lewis said with a grin. "Doesn't seem like much of a way to welcome visitors."

"It is, though," Willie said as Lewis scrubbed the first of the plates, rinsed off sudsy water, and passed it along for drying. "Puts me in mind of old times."

"Your family?"

"Yes. A long time ago now, it seems."

Lewis nodded, then devoted himself to the dishes. Half the plates were put away when Lewis swallowed hard and gazed intently into Willie's eyes. "I was just four when Pa came back from fightin' the Yankees," the boy said. "What was it like?"

"The war?" Willie asked. Lewis nodded. "Seems like you'd ask your papa about that, Lewis."

"Have, Major. Pa don't speak to it much. Makes him sour."

"Wasn't our best time, you know."

"We've had a fight or two here, too. First with Comanches. Later with some renegade hide hunters. I was pretty scared o' the Indians, but then I was just nine. Last time, with the hiders, I held the horses. Lamar got a shot off, but I stayed to cover."

"Smart thing to do."

"Pa never hid, though. He set right out in front o' everybody. Like a general. Afterward the county made him a colonel o' militia, you know."

"I didn't."

"Was that how it was in the war, you and Pa out leadin' the way, chasin' them Yankees from the field?"

"They did most of the chasing at the end, you know, Lewis. And as to leading the way, I learned just how foolish that was when I took a musket ball at Shiloh. Those that survived found good cover and learned not to take chances."

"But all the stories you hear about lines o' chargin' men!"

"There were charges, all right. Whole regiments screaming murder and throwing themselves at the enemy. But of every ten men that charged, three or four fell on the field. It's what prompted Travis Cobb and me to join the cavalry. Your pa was already a horse soldier. We turned to raiding."

"So that wasn't so different from battlin' Comanches."

"No, fighting's never very much different no matter what the time or place or numbers. It's just killing, Lewis. And doing your best to keep from getting shot yourself."

"And it was like that for Pa in the war?"

"Yes," Willie said sadly.

"For you, too?"

"Yes, for me, too," Willie confessed. "Then and after."

"I wasn't goin' to ask about that, Major. We heard some

33

stories. Bobby Cobb calls on Elyssia regular, and he gets letters from his brother Les. Bobby says—"

"You can't believe everything in letters," Willie said, frowning. "Now you'd better get after those plates again. You've still got strays to run down, I hear."

"You'll lend us a hand?"

"My pinto's run down to a nub."

"We got a hundred horses, Major. I'll saddle a good one for you. Pa used to tell how you could outride a cyclone."

"I was younger then," Willie explained. "But I hold my own."

"Bet you do," the boy said, grinning. They then hurried to finish the dishes. And afterward, riding the broken country along the Brazos, Willie breathed in the clear, fine Texas air and felt alive again.

CHAPTER 5

Willie returned from the range an hour short of dusk. Every inch of him ached, and he couldn't avoid groaning a bit as he climbed off the mottled range pony Lewis Slocum had picked out for him. It now seemed days since he'd wiped the plates dry in Elvira's kitchen. Never had a few hours on horseback proven such an ordeal.

"Major, you look done in," Lewis observed as he took charge of the pony. "Guess we shouldn't have given you such a run."

"Sure shouldn't have," Lamar rapidly agreed. "You probably had a long ride to the ranch already. I remember my first time takin' steers to market. Lord, I near rubbed my backside raw."

"Wasn't your doing," Willie told them as he slapped dust from his clothes. "The years have a way of creeping up on a man. Can't be fifteen forever, and I guess it's time I found that out."

"I'll set about gettin' Ma to heat up some water," Lamar said as he turned his mount over to Lewis. "Good soak in a hot tub can be a comfort."

"Would be," Willie said, nodding. "Figure we've time before dinner?"

"You take your soak," Lamar advised. "If dinner's ready 'fore you finish, I'll fetch you a plate myself."

"Thanks," Willie said, trying to mask the suffering each step now brought him. His back felt as if it had been cracked in three places, and one shoulder was so stiff he didn't think he could raise an elbow.

Nevertheless Willie dragged himself inside the house and limped into the washroom. Lamar rolled a wooden tub into the center of the room, then set off to fetch the required hot water. A quarter hour later Willie was soaking in a steamy bath, scrubbing off dust and sweat while the swirling warmth eased his aches. He found himself recalling the Wichita bathhouse where he and Travis Cobb had found comfort after that first long cattle drive back in '66.

All I need's one of those little Kansas gals to rub my back, Willie thought. Yes, their fingers had been magic. It was amazing how they could work the suffering right out of a man.

Knuckles rapped at the washroom door then, and Willie chased the memory from his mind.

"What you need?" he called.

"Major, I brung you some clean clothes," Lewis explained. "I thought you might've soaked enough."

"Bring the clothes on along," Willie suggested. "As to soaking, I imagine a year wouldn't be enough."

Lewis cracked the door open and slid inside. Hill and Hood peered in through the opening, and Willie waved the younger Slocums in as well.

"They were supposed to stay clear," Lewis declared as he draped the clothes over the back of a chair. "Ma told 'em to wash up for dinner, but there's a pump out front and one in the kitchen, too."

"Just wanted to see you was still alive, Major," Hood said shyly. "We never knew a man to take a bath without a ma to make him do it."

Hill nodded his agreement, and Willie grinned.

"Depends on how much of the range he's brought along home with him," Willie explained, scooping up a bit of the grime collected at the rim of the tub.

"I could be mud-caked right down to my gizzard and never take a bath," Hood announced. "You soak too long, your skin wrinkles up and you turn into an old prune-faced toad like Miz Shapcott, the preacher's wife."

"She's wrinkled worse'n old rawhide, Major," Hill added.

"I don't figure bathing regular's done it to her," Willie told the youngsters. "Life out here bends a woman early. More worries 'n comforts, and that's for pure certain."

"You boys didn't come in to visit Major Delamer," Lewis scolded as he poured water into a washbasin. "Now get to scrubbin' them faces and hands. 'Less you want Ma peelin' some hide off you."

"Don't want that," Hood said, hurrying to the basin.

"No, sure don't," Hill agreed, following along.

As the boys washed, Willie dipped his head under the tepid water and rinsed the last of the soap off his face. Lewis handed over a towel. Willie dabbed the water from his eyes and nose, then wearily rose from the tub. As he stepped out, he wrapped the towel around his trim waist and tried to shake off his exhaustion.

"Lord, Major, you're bleedin'," Lewis observed, pointing to the trickle of blood dribbling down Willie's side.

"Is that a bullet hole?" Hood asked, trotting over. "Lew, look at that! He's got scars all over the place."

"Well, Pa told you he fought in the war, didn't he?" Lewis grumbled as he handed Willie a second towel. "Stop starin'. Ain't polite. Anyway, you little ones ought to be helpin' set the table."

"Sure," Hood said, hesitating. "I never seen so many scars, though. Can't all be from the war, either. It's been over a long time now, and that's new blood."

"There's lots o' wars," Lewis announced. "Ain't all of 'em over, either."

The younger boys scampered away as Lewis flashed them an impatient glance. Hood was careful to close the door behind him. Lewis took his turn at the washbasin, then emptied its contents into a drain.

"Sorry if they bothered you," Lewis said as he dragged the tub toward the drain. "Little ones just bound to ask questions, I guess, and those two'll jabber your ear off given half a chance."

"I had a little brother myself," Willie replied as he dried himself. "It can be a vexation, but there's comfort to it, too."

"None I've ever seen," Lewis muttered.

"Oh, I don't know. Feels kind of good somehow, knowing you have brothers who'll stand by you."

"Hood and Hill? They wouldn't be much help in a fight."

"They won't stay small forever, Lewis."

"No, but when they grow up, you can't be sure how they'll stand, can you? Not to hear Jess Cobb speak o' your brother Sam anyhow."

"Isn't often a snake gets himself born to a good family," Willie remarked.

"More'n one prayer's been said to that account," Lewis replied. "Hood's right about one thing, though. That's fresh blood. Might be best if Ma took a look at your side. She's got a way with hurts."

"This one's near mended," Willie argued.

"Yeah?" Lewis said, walking over to take a closer look. "Looks nasty enough to me. Lucky it missed the lung. Clipped a rib, I guess, and bounced out the side. Wasn't the only new one, either. Here's a fresh scar on your shoulder."

"There's one on the leg, too," Willie noted. "Laid me up two weeks and some odd days. A man can't stay abed forever, though."

"And the ones that shot you?"

"They won't be bothering anybody, not ever again," Willie said sourly.

"Meanin' you kilt 'em?"

"I did."

"So that's what you do these days, eh, Major?" Lewis asked as he opened a small cabinet and drew out a strip of cloth. "Kill people? Did Pa send for you then?"

"Got somebody hereabouts needs killing?" Willie asked. Lewis shook his head and passed over the cloth.

"I'll help bind you up," the boy offered, changing the subject.

"Does it bother you, knowing what I've been about?"

38

Willie whispered as he discarded the towels and helped Lewis wrap the bandages.

"Ain't that," Lewis said, concentrating on the bandages and avoiding Willie's probing eyes. "It's just, well, Pa says it's a hard thing, shootin' at another man. Robs your soul, he told Lamar and me once. So I won't say it bothers me exactly. Just makes me sort o' sad. You didn't bring your troubles here with you. I know that. You come to forget, I'd wager."

"Don't know that's possible," Willie said, wincing as Lewis tightened the bindings.

"Pa ain't forgot the war, Major. But he sort o' started over. The Cobbs too. Plenty o' land not claimed in these parts. Man could still build himself a nice ranch."

"You sound like your papa," Willie observed.

"Don't mean it's not true," Lewis said, tying off the bandage. "I'll leave you to get yourself dressed. Ma's bound to start dinner pretty soon. She won't wait on anybody, you know."

"Wouldn't expect her to," Willie said, giving the boy a tap on the shoulder. "You tell her I'll be along directly."

"Sure, Major. You look some better. Guess the bath worked out the wearies."

"Yeah," Willie said, returning the boy's grin. That or the talk, he thought.

The Slocums were in the midst of enjoying plates of beef stew when Willie joined them. Lewis motioned to the empty chair separating himself and Lamar, and Willie walked over and sat there. Platters of food came his way, and he helped himself liberally.

"How's the west range appear, Lamar?" Ted Slocum asked after a bit.

"Dry, Pa," the fifteen-year-old replied. "Stock's collectin' at what's left o' Muddy Creek, but even the deep pools won't last long. I'd guess another week without rain, and won't be nothin' but rocks to drink."

"We'll start movin' 'em tomorrow," Slocum declared. "How're things south?"

"Close to as bad, Pa," Lewis explained. "Bobby Cobb

was out lookin' for better range for their stock, and he said that stretch to the south's parched."

"Then it's north to the river," Slocum said, sighing. "Sound like Texas, Major? Lookin' for water or else duckin' hailstones."

"I'll confess it's familiar," Willie answered. But as the Slocums went on to describe storms and floods that had tormented the country that spring, Willie merely nodded. It was difficult after being alone those past weeks to adjust to so many voices. He didn't know quite how to break in or even what to say. It was easier to nibble a biscuit and listen.

Later, as night settled in, Ted Slocum drew Willie out to the long covered porch.

"I've got two empty rooms out in the bunkhouse, Major," Slocum explained. "I don't keep on a full crew this time o' year, and the men who stay in the third room are off with Gus to Weatherford, all save three or four. Plenty o' room there for a man to stretch out."

"I don't need much," Willie pointed out. "Just room to roll out my blankets."

"Then there's the boys," Slocum said, glancing at the four faces peering guiltily out of the front doorway.

"Yeah?"

"Seems they got it into their heads you need lookin' after. Lewis says he bandaged a wound. Ain't serious, is it?"

"No," Willie said, laughing. "Just bleeds some when I bounce my insides around."

"Like ridin' the range?" Slocum said, frowning.

"More like riding anywhere, Ted. I was warned to rest up another week in Colorado, but you know me. I get the itch to travel, and I have to go."

"I could have Elvira take a look, Major. She's a fair hand as a doc. Folks for fifty miles around call on her at birthin' time, you know, and I lose count o' how many youngsters she's sewed back together."

"This's been patched," Willie explained.

"Was a bullet did it then."

"It was," Willie confessed. "I have a talent for collectin' 'em, you'll recall."

"Ain't the healthiest o' habits, either. Maybe we ought to fix up Gus's room for you. He'll be away a while yet."

"That's not what the boys had in mind, though, was it?"

"No, they thought maybe you'd throw in with them. Lamar and Lewis took a shine to you. That's plain to see. As for the little ones, they got expectations o' war stories and tall tales from the Rockies. It's worse'n a bunkhouse, what with the four o' them squawkin' and stirrin' 'round. I wouldn't wish it on my worse enemy. But if you've gone and lost your senses, they've asked you to take Lamar's bunk. He'll make himself up a mattress o' straw and throw it onto the floor."

"Doesn't seem right to displace him," Willie argued.

"Oh, he's half the time off sleepin' under the stars. Boy doesn't take to roofs. Puts me in mind o' somebody I used to know."

"Does it?" Willie asked.

"So what'd be your choice?"

Willie eyed the door a moment. Lamar and Lewis looked hopeful. The little ones pleaded. It was a fool's move, choosing that madhouse. But after weeks of solitude, he couldn't resist the lure of company.

"Yeah," Slocum said, laughing. "That's the trouble with kids. They don't really leave much choosin' to a man, do they? And the gal's even worse! Lamar, make up your mattress. Major's determined to accept your invite."

"Hooray!" Hood hollered, racing over and grabbing Willie's hand. "You wait'll you see the wolf's hide I got. Pa shot him, but I worked the skin myself."

Hill joined the escort, and Lewis met them at the door. It was hard to make sense of the jabbering, but Willie didn't really mind. There was rare comfort to be found in those boys' admiring eyes, and their attentions were a balm for a troubled soul.

It was later, after a half-dozen tales and a fair sample of pranking, that Willie took to his bed. The others fell asleep quickly, and their restless turning and childish stirrings took Willie back to a world he thought he'd left behind. He remembered the night before he'd ridden off to war. There was Jamie, tossing to and fro, crying out fearfully, and Willie

41

sitting helplessly in a corner, unable to offer comfort or solace.

"What nightmares visit you?" Willie whispered, watching Hood thrash about in the lower berth of the two-tiered bed.

Lamar lay limp as a rag doll, and except for snoring lightly, he might as well have been dead. Hill moved around quite a lot, but he appeared less fitful atop the far bed.

Not so young Lewis. His bare arm had a habit of dangling down from overhead, and his bare feet had already dislodged a blanket. Feet hung over the end of the bed, and Willie worried the boy might slide off the bunk and crash to the floor.

Willie scrambled to his feet, rescued the discarded blanket, and prepared to return it when a voice whispered, "Don't mind him, Major. He's always tossin' off his covers."

Willie turned to find Hood gazing over.

"Shoot, once he even threw off his nightshirt," Hood went on to say, laughing to himself. "Ma come in next mornin' and found him jaybird-naked! I figure that's what turned his hair so white."

Willie nevertheless returned the blanket, then made his way over to Hood and offered the nine-year-old a reassuring pat on the chest.

"Best find your rest," Willie advised. "Day's long and hard on a ranch."

"Yes, sir," Hood replied. "Tomorrow maybe Hill and I'll show you our hogs. We got a couple o' real thumpers. Wait an' see."

"Sure," Willie said, nodding as he turned back toward his own bed. He remained restless, though, and after a bit he pulled on his trousers and walked out onto the porch. Overhead a million stars sparkled in a clear midnight sky. He picked out the constellations and recalled his father's tales of their origins. Then the floorboards behind him creaked, and Willie turned with a start.

"Too noisy?" Ted Slocum called. "Still room in the bunkhouse."

"It's not that," Willie said, sighing. "Or maybe it is. I don't know anymore myself. There's comfort in the little noises kids make at night. Or the touch of a woman at your side. It's just I haven't known either for such a long time, and it's brought on a storm of memories."

"You're close to home, Major."

"Don't you think it's time you started calling me Willie? War's a long time over."

"Is it?" Slocum asked. "For you, I mean? You never did hitch yourself up with Ellie Cobb, after all. And your pa's ranch . . ."

"Sure, I know," Willie mumbled. "War's over just the same. It didn't turn out the way I planned, and nothing has since."

"Didn't have to be that way, Maj . . . Willie," Slocum said with some effort. "I was with Trav when he told her. She'd have waited for you a little longer. She'd have gone anywhere, too."

"I know. I saw her myself a year or so back, and she told me. Named her eldest boy Willie, thinking me dead. That's the worst of it, Ted, knowing I wasn't the only one sad. She's found herself a good husband now, though."

"And you?"

"I'm alive. Not all that easy considering what I've turned my hands to."

"You know, I never could see why you let that snake of a brother have your pa's ranch. All through the war you kept talkin' about gettin' home, buildin' up the place, marryin' Ellie and—"

"You don't have to tell me," Willie cried. "I see it every night in my dreams. But it wasn't that easy. You know Sam sent men to kill me?"

"I know who ended up dyin', too. You should've squared off with that no-account and put an end to him."

"Just what would that have made me?" Willie asked. "Better'n Sam? I would've killed my own brother, not just tried. Would Jamie have admired that? What of Sam's wife and kids? They'd surely admired their papa's murderer."

"So you rode away."

"Couldn't stay without one of us dying, Ted."

"You were wrong, Willie Delamer," Slocum declared.

43

"Sam deserved killin'. And 'cause you left, plenty o' people've suffered. The Cobbs lost their place."

"I saw to it Sam signed a paper guaranteeing their rights," Willie objected.

"Was a fire. And men got shot."

"I couldn't know Sam'd do that."

"Couldn't you? Everyone else did."

"So I made a mistake. Not the first one, you know. Lately seems like I got myself a talent for being wrong."

"So will you visit Sam?"

"No," Willie said, vigorously shaking his head.

"And Trav? He's just a few miles east, you know."

"I don't suppose it's a thing to put off."

"Tomorrow then. Your side's mended well enough?"

"It is," Willie assured his old friend. "I'll be fine if I can catch some rest."

"Won't out here," Slocum pointed out as he turned Willie toward the house. "You can't miss Trav's house. It sits on a hill overlookin' the river. Just like my place."

"Sure," Willie said, accompanying Ted inside the house. "I'll leave after breakfast."

"I could send one o' the boys along with you."

"No, it's a ride best made alone," Willie decided. "And soon."

CHAPTER 6

Willie sat silently at the breakfast table, pondering the re-union that lay ahead. Part of him longed to see Trav again, yearned for the old days when the two of them had dared anything, had hunted and fished and swum away summers twice as hot as that scorcher of '76! But somehow Willie knew things would be different now. The familiar banks and crossings where they'd roamed were now fenced in by brother Sam's stinging wire. Old Art Cobb and Big Bill Delamer, who had nurtured their sons into the best kind of men, were both dead now. And as for the boys, well, war and ten years of hard living had marked Willie Delamer. What might they have done to Travis Cobb?

Willie wondered as he saddled his pinto and rode out east-ward along the river. He noticed his fingers lacked their ac-customed steady grip on the reins. Twice Willie halted the pinto and prepared to turn back. Each time Tatanka Yotan-ka's haunting words raced through Willie's mind. And so he nudged the pinto along those two infernally long miles. At last he spotted the Cobb place.

The house, like Ted Slocum's, sat atop a low hill. The Cobbs had built a long cabin of picket logs. There was a shed of sorts around back for hay and a corral for the horses. Sitting as it was on that bleak, dust-tortured landscape, the place was about as far from Willie's vision of paradise as any he could recall.

Down by the river a pair of young men in their early twenties were filling water barrels. A third, maybe sixteen or seventeen, pointed a wary hand at Willie and called out in alarm.

"Got a rider comin'!" the boy shouted.

Instantly his companions abandoned their chore and fetched rifles from the bed of a nearby wagon.

"Hold it right there!" the oldest of the three men demanded. "State your business!"

Willie drew to a halt and eyed his rifle-toting welcoming committee. It wasn't how anybody would have envisioned a reunion.

"Who are you?" the second man asked, studying Willie's face and observing the dusty gray cavalry hat.

The voice stunned Willie, as did the features. Here was a man certainly no older than what—twenty-one, twenty-two? His dirty brown hair and probing eyes were hauntingly familiar. This was Travis reborn.

The younger of the three was much the same, only his cheeks lacked the dark stubble of his brother's, and his eyes were a bit brighter. Of course, he wasn't cradling a Winchester.

The older one, too, was certainly a Cobb. He was lighter in color, slimmer, and a bit freckled. There was a hint of Ellen in his face, and his fiery eyes brought back a dozen memories.

"What brings you here?" the yellow-haired gunman asked, raising the barrel of his rifle. "This is Cobb land."

"I know," Willie said, sighing. "It's to see Travis Cobb I've come here."

"Go fetch Trav," the eldest instructed the youngest. "And Davy, don't be long at it."

"Won't," the boy pledged as he raced toward the house.

"If he's Davy, you'd be Bobby," Willie said, somberly gazing at the dark-haired young man. "And you," he added, staring at the blond, "have to be Jesse."

"That's right," Jesse said nervously. "Guess you've come

46

to tell us that, have you? Might be smart for you to drop that big Sharps off your horse. And the rifle off the side, too. Then the pistols.''

"Expecting trouble?" Willie asked as he unbuckled his gunbelt.

"You stay in this country long, it happens," Bobby explained as he approached cautiously and took custody of the weapons. "You'll get 'em back when you leave, mister."

"Mister?" Willie said, searching the faces for some hint of the little boys who had once rocked on a knee and listened to tall tales.

"He's no mister," an older voice declared.

Willie turned and stared down at the wrinkled, leathery face of Travis Cobb. An amber-haired wisp of a boy walked alongside. Davy was two steps behind.

"Been a time, Trav," Willie said, extending a hand toward his old friend.

"A lifetime," Travis pronounced as he clamped an iron grip on Willie's fingers and pulled him off his horse. For a moment the two of them stumbled. Then Travis lurched to his left, and the both of them splashed into the river.

"Trav!" Bobby called, swinging his rifle to bear.

"Pa!" the boy screamed as he plunged in after them.

Willie floundered a moment before sinking beneath the surface. He emerged, sputtering and laughing, only to have the boy leap upon his back and begin pounding his shoulders.

"Hold there, Mike!" Travis called, rescuing Willie from the relentless attack. "It's all right, boy. We're old friends, Willie and me."

"Oh," the boy said, smiling sheepishly. "Didn't know, mister. Sorry for thrashin' you."

"*You* are forgiven," Willie told the youngster. "As for Trav here, well, I'm not so sure."

"Keep your hands to your side!" Jesse shouted as Willie fetched his hat from the water. "Don't make any sudden moves."

"Put that rifle down, Jess!" Travis growled. "This here's Willie Delamer!"

"Delamer?" Davy said, paling. "Lord, I thought him dead a half-dozen summers back."

"World'd be better off if he was," Jesse declared. "Ain't a real Brazos man alive'd weep if the whole blamed family choked."

Davy shook his head and muttered. Bobby stared accusingly. Travis flashed a displeased look at his brothers and shook water from his shaggy hair.

"Been a time since we went swimmin' in this fool river," Travis observed. "Sun's high. Won't take long to dry out our clothes."

"There's a deep pool yonder," little Mike declared, pointing to his left.

"And willow limbs for a clothesline," Travis noted. "Well, old friend? Got some Texas dust to wash off you?"

"Sure," Willie said, trying to match Travis's smile.

Willie, Travis, and little Mike splashed their way upstream, slung their clothes over willow branches, and splashed into the river. Jesse and Bobby returned to their labors. Davy, on the other hand, tied the pinto to a willow branch and then joined the swimmers.

"Can't mind Jess," Davy explained, staring at the scars marking Willie's chest and side. "He took Pa's dyin' harder'n anybody, and he blames your brother Sam."

"And don't you?" Willie asked.

"I used to pass some time with Robert, you know," Davy said, gazing eastward with sad eyes. "We were friends, you'd say, even if our families didn't think much o' each other. Ain't seen Robert for better'n two years now. He went down to Austin for schoolin'. Not many boys hereabouts you can shoot rabbits with or take with you to town and hunt up fun."

"No, I'd guess not," Willie said, smiling faintly. "He's a good boy, is he? Robert, I mean."

"Always been a friend to me," Davy answered. "But things can change. Jess says it's best forgotten, us bein' enemies. Was Delamers chased us off our place!"

"I never thought it'd come to that," Willie muttered. "I thought for certain those agreements Sam signed . . ."

"The house caught fire," Travis explained.

"I heard," Willie said, swallowing. "Guess I underestimated Sam. Was a problem I had more'n once."

"Yeah," Travis agreed. It was only now, when Willie climbed up onto the bank, that the others noticed the blood dribbling down Willie's side. Eyes grew wide with alarm, but Willie only shook his head and laughed.

"Just a bit of a leak," he assured them. "I passed the night at Ted Slocum's, and one of the boys wrapped me up in bandages so tight I thought I'd choke. Cut 'em off this morning, and I guess that opened it up some."

"Never saw anybody with so many scars," Davy remarked.

"Not anybody," Mike added. "Even Pa."

"We been in a few fights, eh, Willie?" Travis asked.

"War or two," Willie replied. "But I'd judge you've found something better to do with yourself. Pa, eh?"

"Yeah," Travis said, pulling Mike to his side. "Got myself hitched just before leavin' the old place. Irene's her name. Can't wait for you to meet her. Pretty as a peach, and a worker! Nobody can match her cookin' for a hundred miles."

"Two hundred," Mike boasted.

"But the boy," Willie said, scratching his chin. "You say you married just before leaving the old place. That's just been what, six, seven years?"

"Irene was married before," Travis explained. "So I sort of got Mike here in the bargain, eh, son?"

"That's right," Mike agreed. "Never really had a pa before. My first one got kilt in the war, you see."

"I do see," Willie said as he washed the trickle of blood from his side. "Well, you fell into good fortune when your mama found Trav here."

"More the other way 'round," Travis insisted. "Irene's been a balm, Willie. A good woman's a true comfort."

"Yes," Willie said, nodding sadly as the image of Ellie's face flashed through his mind.

"She writes regular," Travis whispered as he splashed ashore. "If you'd like, you could read the letters."

"Just makes it harder," Willie declared.

"Well, if you change your mind, I've got 'em put by."

49

Willie nodded, then stepped over to the willow. The clothes were still damp, so he sat in the shade and waited for the wind and sun to finish their work. Travis, Davy, and little Mike ambled over shortly, and the four of them swapped stories of rogue mustangs and caught up on the intervening years. Later, when the clothes were finally dry, they dressed and headed up the hill to the picket cabin.

A tall, slender woman with blond hair and delicate features appeared in the doorway.

"Well, he seems friendly enough," she observed. "You might have sent word, you know."

"Sorry, dear," Travis said, motioning her outside. "Irene, this is my oldest friend in this world," he told her. "Willie Delamer."

"Delamer?" she whispered. Then, turning to Willie, she said, "Hello," and reluctantly took his hand.

"Pleased to meet you, ma'am," Willie replied. "It seems Trav's done just fine for himself."

"We're happy," she said, stepping aside.

"Come on, Willie," Travis said then, pulling his old friend along inside. "There's somebody else you should meet."

Actually there were two somebodies. In seven happy years together Travis and Irene had added a pair of boys to their family. The oldest, at five, was walnut-headed Arthur. Named for Travis's father, the boy was the image of his father. Fair-haired Joshua, three, was frail by comparison. The two youngsters nestled shyly under their father's arms when Travis knelt down to greet them.

"It's fine work you've done with 'em," Willie observed. "Good to know all the dreams haven't died."

"Ah, Willie, it's your hat's gray," Travis said, shaking his head. "Not your hair."

Irene provided glasses of cool mint tea, and Travis led Willie back to the porch. The two old friends spent the remainder of the morning there, rocking in a porch swing while Mike entertained Art and Josh a few feet away.

"It's not been altogether easy," Travis admitted after a bit. "We've had the unwelcome attentions of rustlers now

50

and then, and the Comanches paid us a call in '73. Still, we've come through it.''

"But you're wary of strangers," Willie noted.

"Pays to be careful," Travis muttered. "Jesse spotted some riders a day or so back.''

"Fellow with a buggy?''

"No, just riders. You see somebody?''

"Over at Ted's place," Willie explained. "Looked like a railroad surveyor maybe.''

"Railroad's due to pass well south o' here," Travis explained. "Just west some Englishmen have bought up big stretches. Some say they figure to fence off a kingdom o' sorts. Puts me in mind of—''

"Yeah," Willie said, gazing eastward. "One king's enough on the Brazos.''

All was relatively peaceful until lunchtime. Considering the crowded kitchen and the noonday heat, tempers were just bound to flare. Willie was salting a slice of roasted beef, and Jesse suddenly grabbed the small porcelain shaker away.

"Jess?" Travis called angrily.

"What?" the younger man shouted.

"Mind your manners," Travis said nervously. "Willie's our guest.''

"Not mine!" Jesse barked. "Not ever mine. Nor yours, either, Trav. He's a Delamer, ain't he? You forget about Pa? Leavin' that ranch kilt him sure as a bullet through the heart would've done! And here you welcome a Delamer to table, treat him like some long-lost kin!''

"That's just what he is," Travis insisted. "We're brothers in more ways'n you'll ever imagine.''

"He kilt Pa!" Jesse argued.

"That wasn't Willie's doin'," Travis declared, rising angrily to his feet. "I won't have it said otherwise. Willie Delamer's been a better friend to all of us than maybe you'll ever know. Now you bridle that mouth 'fore it brings you harm, hear?''

"I ain't afraid o' him," Jesse grumbled.

"Maybe you should be," Travis countered. "While you been growin' chin hairs, Willie there's been battlin' Yanks

51

and Comanches and all manner o' vermin. Stood by your sister Ellie in Kansas and backed up brother Les out in Colorado. Wouldn't hear a cross word from either o' them about it. Now, there's an end to it. I'll have nothin' more said.''

But if the words weren't spoken, the feelings nevertheless remained. Jesse fumed. Never had Willie read such bitter hatred in a man's eyes. Danger lurked very near.

Willie did his best to ignore Jesse Cobb. You can't, Willie told himself, tell a man of twenty-three anything. It's just a matter of proving yourself. Surely time will temper the anger and sorrow.

''So,'' Travis said when the afternoon heat began to ease its fiery blast, ''you figure to earn your keep, Mr. Delamer?''

''What do you have in mind?'' Willie asked in turn.

''Stock's settled in at the water holes. But I've got some rank ponies need gentlin'. Used to be you had a way with horses.''

''Might be I still do,'' Willie remarked, eagerly following his old friend to the corral. In no time Travis turned a pair of speckled mustangs over, and Willie went to work. Someone had already devoted time to both animals, and Willie had no trouble leading the ponies around the corral, then coaxing them to take bit and saddle.

''Nothing to it,'' Willie declared as he climbed atop the first one. The horse stomped about and shuddered, but it didn't buck. Willie rested his cheek against the animal's neck and whispered to it. He then nudged it into a trot.

The second horse was skittish, but Willie had few problems getting mounted. He whispered to the pony, and when the mustang fought his commands, he bit down on one ear and drove his knees into the animal's ribs. In truth, he figured it was the firm hand on the reins that won the horse over, though.

''Haven't lost the knack,'' Travis observed after Willie rode the mustang around the corral a dozen times.

''Ah, they were both near broke,'' Jesse grumbled. ''You think you can work horses, why not try Stinger?''

''Lord, his side's still bleedin','' Davy objected. ''Stinger's a killer!''

Willie eyed Jesse coldly. So this was the challenge, was it? Well, why not?

"Which one is he?" Willie asked.

"The brown one with the white neck," Jesse announced. "Give him a try, Mr. Horse Tamer."

"Here," Bobby said, offering a rope's end. Willie only shook his head.

Willie dismounted and headed toward the brown horse. It was securely tied to the corral rails, and he had a good look. Stinger's flanks were cut by long thin red lines. Spurs! Willie marched over to the shed and located a bucket of axle grease. He dipped his fingers in the bucket and returned to the corral. As he smeared the grease onto the horse's tender side, Willie sang softly an old Comanche chant. The horse seemed to respond to the tune, and Willie managed to untie its halter and cautiously climb onto Stinger's back.

"He's up!" Bobby cried.

"Won't last," Jesse vowed, tossing a stone at the horse's rump. It struck, and Stinger exploded into action. Moments later the animal began leaping and kicking and angrily trying to fling Willie a hundred directions at once. Willie clung to Stinger's back, chewed on one ear and then the other, gripped a handful of mane, and prayed the fiery mustang would regain its senses. Stinger was relentless, though, and the horse finally drove Willie against the corral and dislodged him.

Willie rolled off the angry horse, landing hard on his side. He coughed a mouthful of dust from his lungs and rolled under the bottom rail to escape a pounding hoof.

"Well, did I tell you?" Jesse shouted.

"He stayed on a fair piece," Davy argued. "Longer'n anybody I ever saw."

"You all right?" Bobby called, helping Willie rise.

"Opened up my side again," Willie muttered. "He's a demon, all right. I'll grant you that, Jess. You give me a week, though, and I'll make him a horse to remember."

"Don't figure you'll be forgettin' him anytime soon," Davy said, laughing as Willie slapped dust from his clothes.

"No, he's left me a mark or two," Willie admitted. "Still, a man's got to earn his supper somehow, eh, Trav?"

The words brought a ring of laughter in response. From everyone save Jesse, that is. Willie noticed and frowned. Some nuts were tough to crack, it seemed.

CHAPTER 7

That evening as Willie lay in the river, soaking off the dust and sweat of an exhausting day, he couldn't help observing the antics of Travis's youngsters. With Mike egging them on, Art and Josh were the equal of any clown act ever to visit the West. Upstream a bit Davy and Bobby raced each other across the narrow river. Jesse, sour-faced as ever, watched from the hillside.

Don't waste your years fretting over what's past, Willie would have counseled. He knew. And Jesse had family, didn't he? Was he so deaf he couldn't hear the laughter?

The race concluded in the shallows only a few feet from where Willie was resting. Davy and Bobby popped to the surface like a pair of corks. Davy flashed Willie a cheerful smile. Bobby frowned.

"Bleedin's gotten worse," he observed. "Looks like you shook up the bindin' some."

"Stinger did," Willie replied. "Me, I just went along for the ride."

"Was low, Jesse jabbin' you to ride that horse," Davy chimed in. "Guess he holds your name against you."

"And you?" Willie asked the others.

"Trav says what's to be happens," Davy answered. "And 'sides, Les was through here a year back. He told me some things."

"Oh?"

"Said you saved his neck up in Colorado Territory. And you kilt a man who was after Jack Trent, Ellie's husband."

"She had a lot o' feelin' for you," Bobby declared. "I recall how it was for you two 'fore the war. And after, too. I never figured why you didn't come for her. Well, we thought you dead, o' course. But you weren't."

"I wondered 'bout that myself," Davy said, probing Willie's eyes in search of an answer.

"She's better off," Willie muttered. "I'd just brought her grief."

"She loved you!" Bobby objected.

"Ain't enough, love. It can get a good woman killed. You don't know how it was for me, driftin' in and out o' railroad towns, then winterin' in the high country. Up there your tears'd freeze right on your face. I was with some good men. Two women were along. I was the only one lived to see summer."

The three of them shared a moment of silence. Then Mike cried out, and Willie instantly turned in that direction. The thirteen-year-old was racing to Travis's side, waving something in his hand.

"You ought to show that to your uncle Willie," Travis advised. "Ain't a man I ever met who knows more 'bout the tribes'n he does."

The boy met Willie on the bank and passed over a small sliver of an arrowhead. It was most likely part of a bird arrow, lost in the river or discarded by a band camping nearby. Willie turned the arrowhead over in his fingers a minute, then returned it to Mike.

"You think maybe it's Comanche?" Mike asked.

"Could be," Willie admitted. "This was their hunting country in the summer."

"Tell 'em how you rode with Yellow Shirt," Travis urged.

"Yellow Shirt?" Mike asked. "Who's he?"

"Fiercest chief ever to visit Texas," Travis declared. "Pa and Willie's pa fought him tooth and nail for what, ten years? Then they made a peace o' sorts. Willie went to the buffalo hunt with 'em one summer. Only white man I ever heard o' doin' that.''

Willie gazed into their spellbound eyes. He was about talked out, what with swapping memories and spinning tales at the Slocum place. He nevertheless crept up the hill, pulled on his clothes, and told of the skinny white boy who had ridden to the buffalo hunt with Yellow Shirt's Comanches. He showed off the faint scar left by Red Wolf's lance. He told of spirit prayers and buffalo ghosts. He left out the sadder tale . . . of Yellow Shirt's death at the hands of a German farm boy and how Red Wolf was shot to pieces by a band of cowboys. All that came later—after the war that had mangled and distorted everything.

''I seen some buffalo down on the southwest range,'' Bobby declared. '' 'Course some hide hunters'll likely finish 'em. Weren't but twenty.''

''I never tasted buffalo,'' Davy said. ''Had some a hunter claimed he jerked, but it tasted like stringy longhorn beef. I'd bet he was lyin'.''

''We could shoot one,'' Bobby suggested. ''Hide'd make good winter coats for the little ones.''

''It's a thought,'' Travis said, scratching his head. ''Willie?''

''Not much to it,'' Willie muttered. ''Winchester makes it easy, and my Sharps'd drop one 'fore he even knew you was comin'.''

''Not that way,'' Travis said, shaking his head. ''The old way. Like you and I did that summer o' '61, 'fore we marched to Shiloh.''

''It's been a time,'' Willie told them. ''I don't remember all the prayers, and I haven't got a pipe.''

''I've got one o' Pa's old briers,'' Travis explained. ''And tobacco. We'll make do.''

''Please?'' Mike pleaded.

''He's too young,'' Willie announced.

''He's seen men fight and die,'' Travis argued. ''He can ride behind me on my horse. Bobby and Davy'll come, won't you, brothers?''

''Sure,'' Bobby cried.

"Yeah," Davy added. "I'll ride to the Slocum place and invite them along. Gus'll want in."

"He might not be back from Weatherford," Willie explained.

"Oh, he's back," Davy declared. "Rode through this mornin' to grab some o' Irene's cookin'."

"Looks like we're takin' a regular army," Willie said, frowning.

"I'll ask Jess, too, if it's all right?" Bobby asked. "He's sour as death, I know, but he's got a shooter's eye."

So do I, Willie thought to answer.

They headed out at dawn the next morning. Willie and Bobby Cobb led the way. Travis followed, with Mike bobbing along behind him. Davy Cobb rode alongside Lamar and Lewis Slocum. Their father and tall, shaggy-haired Gus Slocum accompanied Jesse Cobb at the tail of the procession.

Willie felt the eyes of the others on his back. Jesse continued to brood, and Gus Slocum was perplexed by the notion that shooting buffalo required ceremonies and prayers.

"I shot plenty o' things in my time," Gus had complained earlier. "Pa, this's crazy."

"If it's the major's way, best listen and learn," Slocum had advised. "He knows things."

"Knows how to make a muddle o' simple matters," Jesse had added. "Ain't that just like a Delamer."

But the younger Slocums had been downright excited at the notion of riding to the buffalo hunt Indian-style. Lewis actually wore an old buckskin shirt traded off a Tonkawa scout from Fort Griffin. They joined in the prayers and quickly picked up the Comanche chants Willie sang.

"Wasn't so long ago you'd happen across a band or two of Quannah's people out here," Travis told Willie as they watched the younger members of the company ride out to locate the small herd. "Couple o' years now since they stirred up any real trouble. Like as not the ones who'd fight you starved out on the llano. I can remember when you just whispered 'Comanche' and half a town'd head for cover."

"I remember those hard times, too," Willie said, gazing

off into the distance as if he might see the ghosts of those times ride by. "Sam lost a boy to 'em. I think that's what turned him sour on people. Charlie was his particular favorite. I lost a brother young, you recall. Touches a man to bury little ones."

"We've lost a lot o' friends over the years," Travis noted. "But neither of us ever took it into his head to run our neighbors off their property. Or shoot 'em in the night. It takes a hollow-hearted man to shoot bullets at women, at little kids. Or to hire his brother kilt."

"Guess so," Willie admitted. "But I didn't ride out here to talk about Sam. Best set Mike on your horse. The buffs are close by. I feel 'em."

Indeed they were. Willie had scarcely climbed atop the pinto when Lamar Slocum rode by to announce the herd found.

"Lew's watchin' 'em, Major," the fifteen-year-old called. "I already found Jess and Bobby. Th'others won't be far."

"Where are the buffs?" Travis asked as Lamar started to leave.

"Mile and a half west by south, out where Stubble Creek peters out," Lamar explained. "Sittin' and chompin' grass like there's no tomorrow. Guess there won't be for some of 'em."

Lamar then left. Willie gazed at Travis and asked, "Know the place?"

"Been there a thousand times," Travis answered. "I'll lead the way."

By midday the hunters had assembled on a slope overlooking the buffalo. It wasn't much of a herd—just six bulls, ten cows, and a half-dozen calves. They appeared thin for late summer, and Willie decided they'd been on the run a lot. Otherwise they'd have a few more pounds.

"Who takes the shots?" Gus Slocum called as he pulled his rifle from its scabbard. "Jess and I've got the best eyes, I'd wager."

"We'll have half of 'em down 'fore you blink," Jess boasted.

"Didn't come out to murder the whole lot," Travis said,

eyeing the others. "Was to learn how it was back when. We got plenty o' beef to eat. I won't have buffalo carcasses rottin' so somebody can brag on his shootin'."

"It's for the youngsters to shoot," Slocum declared. "I'd say Mike's a bit young, so that leaves Lewis and Lamar, Davy and Bobby."

"Ought to be Lewis," Davy said, swallowing his own disappointment. "He's got the war shirt, and he chants better'n the rest o' us."

"Pa?" Lewis asked. "Major?"

"Take the shot," Travis said, grinning at the white-haired youngster. "Don't miss, though."

Willie dismounted, secured his horse to a juniper limb, and bid Lewis do the same. The others did likewise, and Willie led the way toward the grazing buffalo. The animals ignored their approaching attackers, and Willie found it easy to set up the shot. Lewis knelt, fixed a young bull in his sights, and fired. The Winchester whined, and its bullet tore into the bull's shoulder and pierced its heart. The great hairy beast tottered and fell.

"We could kill two," Bobby suggested.

"We could kill twenty," Willie replied. "Meat'd rot, of course. But it's for each man to decide for himself." Travis and Slocum scowled, and the others fought the urge to fire at the remaining beasts. Gradually the animals moved away, and Willie approached the fallen bull.

Now the hard part begins, he told himself. Skinning the hide and butchering the meat turned many a buff hunter from the trade, and the boys soon tired of the chore. The blood and gore was too much for little Mike, who set off to wade in the creek instead. Lewis, on the other hand, considered himself responsible for the kill and wouldn't shy from the blood or the smell.

"I've butchered beef, you know," the boy explained as Willie pulled a section of ribs from the carcass. "Gelded horses, too. Ain't exactly got the heart for that work, you know, but the livery in Albany won't have stallions. Too wild for most riders, I guess. Sure am glad nobody rides people. Ain't too excitin' a notion, havin' yourself changed."

"Guess not," Willie said, laughing at the faces Lewis made.

They then concentrated on the butchering and left the talk for another time.

Ted Slocum took in hand the building of a fire and the broiling of thick buffalo steaks. The long rid. and the brief hunt had built a powerful hunger in man and boy alike, and the aroma of cooking meat drew even sour-faced Jesse to the fire.

"This is how men ate when the world was young," Slocum declared as he passed a thick steak to Travis. "You'll never taste the equal."

Actually, though, most of the meat was tough and stringy, but its flavor offset each complaint.

"We'll split the rest amongst us," Slocum announced when each person had stuffed himself past reckoning. "Best get it along home 'fore it spoils. The hide's for Art and Josh. That's decided."

"If Willie'll show me how, I'll work it," Davy volunteered.

"I'll help," Mike offered.

"Then everything's settled," Travis announced. "Time we headed home."

"Pa, if you don't need me to haul meat, I'll swing down and see how the stock are doin' on that east range," Gus Slocum said as his father tied a meat bundle onto Lewis's horse.

"I'll come along," Lamar volunteered.

Meanwhile Travis turned Mike and the meat over to Davy.

"Might's well ride the south boundary while we're out here," Travis told the others. "Gus thought he saw a campfire out that way this mornin' on the way to our place."

"I saw somethin' myself," Bobby remarked. "Didn't think much about it, but there were some tracks up that way."

"What manner of tracks?" Willie asked.

"Ruts, like they were left by a wagon. Some horses, too."

"Sure it was a wagon, Bobby?"

"Was wheels," Bobby said, scratching his forehead. "Small cart maybe."

"Or a buggy?" Willie asked.

"Sure, it must've been. A buggy and some men."

"Your surveyor?" Travis asked.

"Would seem likely," Willie agreed. "Maybe we ought to take a look."

"You leave us to handle our own business," Jesse barked. "Bobby, we'll ride off and see to it ourselves. You with me?"

"Sure, big brother, but I don't see it'd hurt to have some more company."

"How 'bout it?" Trav asked. "Willie and I've been through a few scrapes in our time, Jess."

"So we've heard a thousand times. Ain't babies need protectin', Trav. We'll have a look and ride back with word o' what it is."

"Willie?" Travis asked.

"Boy's got to take his first man steps sometime," Willie observed.

"Then we'll see you for supper," Travis said, bidding farewell to his brothers. "Don't be late."

"Never for food," Bobby said, laughing as he urged his horse into a trot.

"Never!" Jesse agreed.

"I'll wish I'd gone along by the time we get home," Travis said afterward.

"Sure, you will," Willie agreed. "But Jesse's bound and determined to prove himself. We weren't any different, you know. Wasn't it why we mustered into the army?"

"Sure, I know. We were fools, though, Willie, and nigh got ourselves kilt."

"Want I should trail 'em?" Willie asked. "I'd be a shadow. They'd never know."

"No, you've still got a side to mend. Let's get along home 'fore Davy and Mike've told all the story. I think there's some o' Irene's peach pie left."

"Then what're we waiting for?" Willie asked, kicking the pinto into a gallop. Travis was soon at his side, and the two old Confederates raced each other back to the dusty picket cabin that was home.

CHAPTER 8

As Irene set the dinner plates on the heavy oak table, Willie began to fret. Jesse and Bobby hadn't returned.

"Ain't the first time," Davy noted as he carried in a platter of vegetables. "Two of 'em's likely off pesterin' Elyssia Slocum."

"Trav?" Willie asked.

"It's happened before," Travis confessed. "Never were two fellows with less of a head for time."

Travis slowly tapped his toe on the floor, and his hands had grown moist. He, too, was worried.

When the Cobb brothers still hadn't returned at dusk, Travis could stand it no longer.

"Care to take a ride, Willie?" Travis asked.

"Wouldn't mind," Willie answered. "Figure we might have a look southwest?"

"Thought so," Travis said, studying his friend's anxious gaze. "Why?"

"Look," Willie said, pointing to where a faint yellow pinprick of light glowed on the distant horizon. "That'd be our surveyor friend. Or whatever he is. I'd guess Jesse and Bobby found 'em easy enough."

"Yeah," Travis agreed. "Guess I was a fool to let 'em ride there alone."

"You said it yourself, Trav. Time for 'em to take their man steps. Anyway, I don't figure 'em to've come to much harm."

"You don't know Jesse," Travis said nervously. "He's one to kindle tempers or fuel a fight."

Willie didn't voice his own concerns. They'd hardly bring comfort to Travis Cobb.

Within ten minutes the two old friends were riding out into the twilight. Willie wore his twin pistols, and the Winchester was in its scabbard at his side. Travis carried a rifle, too. They didn't speak of the weapons, nor of the trouble that might lie ahead. It wouldn't be their first battle. They knew.

Less than a mile from the picket house Willie heard horses. He motioned for silence, then cautiously picked his way toward the sounds. He hoped to discover Jesse and Bobby, perhaps laughing about the fine time they'd shared with Elyssia Slocum.

"Take it slow," Travis cautioned. "Could be unfriendly types."

Willie breathed deeply, then slowly exhaled. He hoped not. And in the end he spotted two riderless animals drinking from a shallow pool.

"The paint's Bobby's," Travis announced as Willie collected the ponies. "The chestnut belongs to Jess."

"Then there's surely been trouble," Willie muttered, turning back toward the distant flame. "Well, let's have a look."

They only got halfway to the campfire. Willie was leading the way through a narrow ravine when Travis called him to a halt.

"Over there!" Travis shouted, turning his horse toward a shadowy figure half-hidden in a tangle of junipers. Willie drew out his rifle and observed the scene. Instead of bushwhackers, the figures turned out to be Travis's missing brothers.

"Lord, Trav, it's good to see you!" Bobby cried as he stumbled out into the open.

"Had some trouble?" Travis asked as he dismounted. By then Willie had the other horses there. Jesse wasted no time mounting his. His eyes were red and swollen, and there was a fever wrinkling his brow.

"I'll show 'em!" Jesse vowed.

"Now you just hold up a minute!" Travis barked. Jesse was lathered up and ready to go at somebody, and Willie Delamer happened to be handy. Jesse let fly a torrent of curses as he related his nightmare treatment at the hands of the buggy-riding stranger.

Travis examined his brothers in the faint light. Bobby's face was battered considerably, and his ribs were bruised. Jesse had a slice taken out of his left forearm, and his chest was scratched in a dozen places.

"Who are they?" Travis demanded angrily. "Don't they know they're on my land? How dare 'em!"

"Easy," Jesse said, saving the bitterest pill for last. "I never saw a one of 'em, Trav. Their leader was a funny fellow that talked like he was maybe from England or such. As for the others, I guess they were just range cowboys. Still, they didn't seem the types to chew dust and dodge horns."

"Tell Trav about the horses," Bobby urged. "The brands."

"What brand was on the horses?" Travis asked.

"Oh, a real familiar one," Jesse said, gazing hatefully at Willie. "That funny little fork with the three teeth."

"The trident brand," Bobby explained. "They were Delamer hands, Trav."

"No man can be that greedy!" Travis stormed. "Isn't it enough he's swallowed half o' Palo Pinto County?"

"Maybe there was a fallin' out 'tween Sam and some o' his men," Jesse suggested. "Or he could be helpin' this Englishman out to get himself a favor or two in return."

"Possible," Trav grumbled. "Doesn't really matter. Either way I'll see they pay!"

"What do you have in mind?" Willie asked as Travis drew his rifle from its scabbard.

"What else?" Travis asked. "We'll ride down there and kill 'em."

"Where?" Willie asked. "Do you know how many of 'em

there are? What guns they carry? Is the Englishman the real boss?''

"Doesn't matter," Travis said, shaking his head. "No man's comin' onto my land and beatin' on my family without payin' a high price for it.''

"Slow down a minute," Willie said, blocking Travis's trail. "Raiding's one thing, but I won't see a friend ride into a slaughter pen.''

"Who asked you?" Jesse howled. "You're probably in on it yourself.''

"Hush!" Willie growled. The anger had finally vaulted onto his face, and his grim eyes silenced Jesse. "Trav?''

"Don't you see that I have to go?" Travis asked. "Wasn't so long ago you'd've led us.''

"Got half of you shot, too," Willie added. "There's a better way. A man or even five getting shot's not stopping this. We've got to find out who's back of it.''

"We know," Jesse argued. "I do anyhow.''

"You don't know beans!" Willie responded. "You watch 'em if you want, Trav. Post a night guard. Send word to Ted as well. But you leave the rest to me.''

"But . . .''

"Trust me to tend to this," Willie pleaded. "I'll ride into town and find out everything that's known about this Englishman. Then we'll find his weak spots and make him pay.''

"I don't know," Travis said, pondering the problem.

"I tell you he's in on it!" Jesse complained.

"No, Willie knows what he's about. Best swallow the anger and get along with chores. It's what I aim to do.''

"Trav?" Jesse called in disbelief.

"There's plenty o' time for the other," Travis explained. "Ain't there, Willie?''

"Sure," Willie agreed.

Travis waited for his brothers to pull themselves up onto their horses. Then he turned and led the way homeward. Willie let Bobby and Jesse pass by before pulling into line.

"This ain't over," Jesse muttered angrily when Willie stared at the young man's battered face.

"No, I'd say not," Willie agreed. "But I'm not an enemy, Jesse. You'd do yourself a favor by not making me one."

Willie spent an anxious night at the Cobb place. Travis offered to throw a straw mattress on the floor of the small room shared by Mike and the little ones, but Willie preferred the solitude of the shed. After the closeness he'd felt at the Slocum place and the excitement that had filled the Cobb house before the buffalo hunt, the silent barn proved a trial. Still, it did offer Willie a chance to set his mind on the task that lay ahead.

Dawn found him saddling the pinto for the ride into the new county seat of Shackleford County. Albany, they'd named the town.

"It's a far cry from the Flat," Travis declared as he passed over a pair of biscuits and a flour sack of food for later on. "Irene's put out you won't stay for breakfast."

"Better I'm off early," Willie explained. "For what I plan, it's best not too many folks're around to take notice."

"And what is it exactly you'll be doin'?" Travis asked.

"Looking through the county plats," Willie explained. "The deeds and records. Anybody buying up land will show up in the records, don't you suppose?"

"You figure that's what that fellow with the buggy's up to?"

"Don't you? Why else'd he be on your range? He's looking for crossings, Trav."

"I told you the railroad's going' south o' here."

"Sure," Willie said, nodding. "Pretty soon ranchers'll be shipping their stock at the railheads, too. How do they get the stock there? Across the Brazos. Lot of country to the north opening up. The man who controls the river crossings can set tolls, make a fair penny."

"That's true enough," Travis said, frowning. "You know, Willie, when the river rises in late spring, there aren't many good crossings. Three, in fact."

"Where?"

"One's in the shadow o' Fort Griffin, there where the Tonkawas have their camp."

67

"And the others?"

"One's on Ted's acreage. Th'other's yonder," Travis added, pointing to the bend in the Clear Fork of the Brazos just beyond the shed.

Willie stared at the river peacefully churning along. One of the ironies of frontier life was that water, the source of life, so often proved to be the bone of contention for warring factions. So now was this likely to be the case. He hoped to find the answer in the dusty ledgers and plat books of Albany.

CHAPTER 9

Travis had been generous in describing Albany. Settled by a pair of brothers after the war and named for the Georgia home of a merchant, the town consisted of a mercantile store, a pair of houses, a grog shop, livery, and jailhouse. The latter doubled as county courthouse, and it was there that Willie took his questions.

"What do you want with the plat book?" a sleepy clerk asked when Willie roused him from a midmorning nap. "Ain't but half the county deeded, you know, and I can tell you who owns near every parcel."

"Then maybe you could tell me if anyone's bought the acreage adjoining Ted Slocum's TS Ranch," Willie countered. "And exactly how much of that land might be held by the same man."

"County owns a stretch of it," the clerk explained. "Figure to put a road there one day. As to the rest," he said, scratching behind one ear, "I'm not altogether sure."

"Then maybe I could see the plats?" Willie asked.

"Oh, I know what the book says," the clerk said, smiling shyly. "Raymond Tyler owns one section. Another's held by Nathan Barclay. Then there's Andrew Stratford, Walter West, and so on."

"Can't be that many involved," Willie muttered.

"Ain't," the clerk said, grinning. "Names can tell you a

lot sometimes, though. We had an Indian raid back in what—
'71 I think it was. A party o' buffalo hunters holed up close
to a week 'tween here and the Flat. Five got 'emselves kilt."

"Let me guess," Willie mused. "Tyler, Barclay . . ."

"Didn't figure you to come by that gray hat by accident.
Man gets himself through a war and lives ten years besides
has to have a head to go with them twinned sidearms. Don't
suppose you happened to ride with Ted Slocum up in Virginia, did you? Nor hold a major's braid when all was said
and done."

"And if I did?" Willie asked nervously.

"Then you might've known a boy named Franklin Little."

"I did," Willie said, dipping his chin and trying to fight
off the haunting face of young Frank Little. "I buried him
after Five Forks. He was just seventeen. War was close to
over."

"Ted told me you'd passed through," the clerk said so-
berly. "Frank was my youngest. His brothers died fightin'
Sherman in Georgia. All I got now's a tadpole of a grandson.
Boy likes to ride horses with Mike Cobb and the Slocum
boys."

"I liked Frank," Willie said, shuddering. "He wasn't with
us long. Six months. The agony at Petersburg and the scramble to get clear from Richmond."

"He wrote me a letter, mentioned you considerable."

"Mr. Little, if there's anything I can ever do for you . . ."

"Seems to me maybe the shoe's on the other foot, Major," Little observed. "Maybe I can do a thing or two for
you. And for Ted and Cap'n Cobb."

"You seem to know an awful lot," Willie noted. "I'd hate
to have you on the other side, sir."

"Well, that's as fine a compliment as I've had in a week.
The world's run by file clerks, you know. So far's Shackleford
County's concerned, I know it all. What can I tell you?"

"These phony names," Willie began. "Do you know
anything about the man behind them? Who filed the deeds?"

"He was an Englishman," Little explained. "Pair of 'em
really. One old. Other was kind of on the youngish side. Son

70

o' the first, I'd guess. They can put down any old name on the plat, but I didn't notice 'em passin' on the deeds to anybody.''

"And which sections have they bought?"

"What was left along the Clear Fork, from the edge o' Tonkawa camp to where the TS starts. Then north toward the Red River and south to town.''

"Sounds like they plan on putting a trail of their own through,'' Willie said, frowning.

"They'll need a high water crossin' for that. The county's got claims on the Tonkawa ford. That leaves . . .''

"Yes, it does,'' Willie agreed.

"I'm not a man for volunteerin' information all the time,'' Little continued, "but if somebody asked, I might have a bit more to say as regards these land purchases.''

"Such as?"

"The first three sections were bought with cash, Major. Yank greenbacks. The last one was paid by bank draft.''

"What bank?" Willie inquired.

"First Texas Bank o' Jacksboro.''

"Then it wasn't any ghost signed the draft.''

"Signed Romney Fairchild, as I recall.''

"Yes, Fairchild,'' Willie said, recalling the name from his earlier encounter with the man. "Being an observant man, Mr. Little, what else might you know about this English gentleman?''

"Wouldn't bend over backward callin' him a gentleman for one thing. He's been stayin' at Miss Myra Brook's place over at the Flat. Heard how he roughed up one o' Miss Myra's gals. Ain't much for losin' at cards, either, to hear folks talk.''

"Oh?" Willie asked.

"Doesn't do anything about it himself, mark you. But he's never far from those gun hands o' his.''

"Just how'd he come to hire on help?"

"You might be knowin' more 'bout that than me,'' Little replied. "No secret those fellows rode range for your brother till June.''

"And when did Fairchild arrive?"

" 'Bout that same time," Little explained, busying himself with some papers. "Don't know there's any connection, understand, but folks deem it peculiar."

"Folks aren't always wrong," Willie declared. "I appreciate the opportunity to visit with you, sir. Might be I happen along again one day. And if I don't, you can always pass along word to the Slocums. We won't be far from earshot, the bunch of us."

"That'd be a good notion, I'm thinkin', Major. So, you'll ride out to the Flat now?"

"Best way to find out about a man's to take a look at his camp," Willie pointed out.

"Just watch out you don't walk into a nest o' rattlers. There's a couple o' them hands know their business."

"Yeah?" Willie asked. "I know mine, too."

Now wasn't the time for confrontation, though. Willie had learned the hard way you didn't square off against a man until you knew him. And that he was the one that mattered. Mike Dunstan had hammered that lesson into Willie's head.

"Go for the head," Dunstan had preached down on the Cimarron. "Chop off the payroll, and the others'll see there's no profit left in the fight."

It had worked on the Cimarron, and a dozen times later. And Willie had a more personal reason for determining whether or not Romney Fairchild was behind this new trouble. If he wasn't, clearly Sam Delamer was!

Haven't you stolen enough, Sam? Willie silently asked as he mounted the pinto and rode north toward Fort Griffin and the Flat. Can't you be content knowing you robbed my home and my future, ran the Cobbs and who knows how many other good people off land they bled to tame?

Sam Delamer would have laughed at such sentiments. His was a new breed of rancher—a man who was all eyes and greedy paws. And lacking a conscience!

It was only fifteen miles or so north to Fort Griffin. It vexed Willie some to have come so far south just to turn around and head north again. And yet he knew he'd gotten the first clues toward solving the mystery of Romney Fairchild. The next were to come late that afternoon when Willie strolled through the swinging doors of Myra Brooks's house of amusements.

"Howdy," a girl of delicate complexion and pain-hardened eyes called as he stepped toward a pair of planks laid atop flour barrels. "Never you mind the bar. Come along with me. We'll have somethin' sent along to tent number three."

Willie gazed into the girl's dead eyes and frowned. From the neck down she looked twenty. Her lithe body twitched and swayed, but Willie hardly noticed. He was transfixed by those eyes. They were a mirror to his own.

She stepped away. She sees it, too, Willie thought. There was a brief unspoken understanding. Then she turned to greet another newcomer, and Willie set about his duties.

"Got anything cold?" Willie asked a heavily bearded man tending the makeshift bar.

"Got some beer ain't altogether hot," the bartender answered. "Give her a try? Just four bits."

Willie nodded, and the bartender filled a glass from a large keg. Willie slapped fifty cents on the planks and took the mug. The beer was warm, but it washed some of the dust from his throat, and he finished it in three long gulps.

"Another?" the bartender asked.

"No, that'll do for now," Willie responded. "Can a fellow find a game of cards anywhere in this town?"

"Are you a player then?" a young, well-dressed man in his midtwenties asked with a strong British accent. "There's always a game to be had when fresh money arrives in Fort Griffin Town. George, won't you find us some cards?" the young man asked a tall cowboy. "I imagine Leon and Ty would like to join us, too."

"Your game's too rich for me, Boss," one of the cowboys answered. The other, a sandy-haired rogue named Leon Martley, sat beside the young Englishman. After a few moments the man named George appeared with three fresh decks of playing cards and Romney Fairchild.

"Father, this gentleman has consented to let us have a try at his fortune," the younger Fairchild announced.

"Has he?" Fairchild Senior asked. "I believe we met on

73

the trail, sir. I'm Romney Fairchild. This is my son Andrew.''

"They call me the Major," Willie countered.

"So you served in the late rebellion," the elder Fairchild observed. "Many in my native land would have supported your cause. England would certainly have recognized the Confederacy had not the moralists in the press interfered."

"All that's been finished ten years," Willie observed.

"Not everyone down here believes that," young Fairchild replied. "We've met a number of staunch Southerners since arriving in New Orleans. And if you were ready to forget, I suppose you'd replace that weathered hat, sir."

Willie managed a grin. It was true enough. But coming from that sly pup, it had the jagged edge of a dagger.

"Let's play cards," Martley suggested. "Have a sit down, won't you, Major. Cut for deal?"

"Sure," Willie agreed. Martley shuffled the cards, and each man cut the deck once. Willie produced a queen of clubs. Andrew Fairchild turned up the ace of hearts.

It was an omen of things to come. The Fairchilds had a talent for shaving cards. Whether they were ranchers or land speculators or henchmen for Sam Delamer now, at one time they had practiced a different trade. A man with quick fingers made a good living on the Mississippi River. If he didn't cross the wrong man, he did just fine on the frontier—especially in a lawless hole of a town like the Flat.

It took Willie close to an hour and more than forty dollars' cash to tumble to their game. It was cleverly done. For one thing, Andrew had a gift for palming cards. His father played straight most of the time, but he could occasionally slip a card in off the bottom of the deck. But all that was secondary. Somehow the Englishmen had steamed off the seals and marked the deck. Oh, they didn't actually place any marks. No, it was done with subtle notches—little scratches an untrained eye never would have suspected. Willie Delamer had passed through too many railheads and gold camps, though. He knew every trick.

The Fairchilds were careful at the way they went about it. They split the winnings between themselves and Martley.

And when the pot wasn't too big, they let Willie take a hand or two.

Time to turn the tables, Willie thought as he took his turn at dealer.

"Seven-card stud?" he asked the others.

They laughed to themselves. It was regarded by serious players as a losers' game. If five cards wouldn't get the job done, would seven?

Willie watched with grim satisfaction as the others built good hands. He skillfully covered his hold card to conceal the ace of clubs. At the bottom of the deck awaited a second ace. Meanwhile he drew a third nine to match a pair.

"Three of a kind," Andrew noted. "The bet is yours, Major."

Willie painted a worried look on his face. Andrew, on the other hand, fought the temptation to laugh. He held the winning cards—a heart flush. His father saw it and bumped Willie's raise. Martley threw in ten dollars, and Willie finally called the bet at an even hundred.

"Deal the final round," Romney Fairchild urged, and Willie placed another card facedown. Except for the concealed ace of diamonds, the cards meant nothing. Of course, the twin aces meant everything. Willie knew as much when he stacked his last ten dollars alongside the pot and called the bet.

"Lord, would you look at this!" Myra called. "I'll bet there's half a thousand dollars on that table."

"Eight hundred twenty by my estimate," the elder Fairchild announced as he turned over his cards. Two pairs wouldn't win that day, though. Andrew revealed his flush. Martley shook his head and tossed his cards in. When Willie slid his three nines over and prepared to reveal the aces, his companions paled.

"Full house!" Myra shouted in awe as Willie revealed the cards. "My word. He's beaten the gents!"

"Has he?" Andrew asked, nodding toward Martley. The cowboy started to rise, then halted. The cold hard barrel of Willie's Colt jabbed into Martley's side.

"He dealt," Romney Fairchild pointed out. "You all saw how he . . . he . . ."

"What is it I did, mister?" Willie asked, drawing the second pistol and resting it on the table. "Eh? You wouldn't say I dealt seconds, would you? I couldn't hold a candle to you boys for that talent."

"Take that back!" Andrew stormed.

"Well, I'll admit you lack your father's mastery, Andy my boy," Willie said, raking the winnings toward him with the pistol. "Nice work on those cards, though. How in the world did you scuff 'em like that and fix the seal on the pack? Maybe you'll teach me that game."

"You won't live that long," Andrew vowed.

"Oh, now you've gone and scared me," Willie said, frowning grimly. "Myra, you'd do an old soldier the favor of putting my winnings in a sack for me, wouldn't you?"

"I can't afford to . . ." she began.

Willie jabbed his pistol into Martley, and the Texan cried, "Do it, honey! For Gods sake, do it!"

Myra collected the money in a flour sack, which Willie tied to his belt with one hand while holding a pistol on the players with the other. He then tipped the house generously and backed out of the place.

Willie bounded along the street to where the pinto was tied. He nearly got there when the first shot splintered a barrel beside his left hip.

So, it's to be a fight, is it? Willie asked himself. He ducked behind a wagon and watched a pair of cowboys charge up the street, firing as they came. Willie took a deep breath, cocked both pistols, and returned the shots. His first shot struck the lead cowboy just above the left eye and dropped him like a stone. The second went wide. Willie watched nervously as the gunman threw himself behind a watering trough.

Oh well, I've only been shooting left-handed three months now, Willie consoled himself.

With just the one attacker, Willie set aside the second pistol and readied himself for a fresh charge. It came, but not from the expected direction. Instead the big man, George, fired a rifle from across the street. The bullet slammed into the bed of the wagon only half a foot from Willie's head. Willie uttered a cry and held his fire. George stepped into the street.

Your last mistake, Willie thought as he shot the cowboy through the chest.

"That's the finish for me!" the man at the trough yelled as he turned and raced away. Willie took a final glance up the street before stepping to the pinto. He secured the money sack, then cautiously mounted. He almost missed seeing Andrew Fairchild.

Willie swallowed hard and readied himself. Young Fairchild stood fifty feet away, aiming a double-barreled shotgun in Willie's direction. Neither hammer was cocked, though. The gun had probably rested back of the bar. Uncocked, it was harmless.

"Don't do it," Willie warned. "There's been enough."

"Have a go at him, son!" Romney Fairchild urged, and Andrew trotted out and pressed both triggers. Realizing his mistake, he set down the shotgun and drew the hammers back with his thumb. The shotgun exploded, taking young Fairchild's face with it.

"Lord Almighty!" Myra screamed.

"Andrew!" Fairchild called.

Willie stared coldly at the old man before riding away.

CHAPTER 10

Willie didn't return to the Cobb place right away. He had some scouting yet to do, and he needed to work the sting and blood of battle out of his system. He rode through the hills, making note of springs and creeks. Fairchild had chosen his property well. It was well-watered acreage. Another man might have built a fine place there. Willie knew Romney Fairchild better now, though. The man was no builder.

Even if he had been, that was bound to change now. Willie couldn't erase the ghastly sight of young Andrew from his thoughts. How would the boy's father do it? No, the fires of vengeance burned hot. Willie knew. He had scars to prove it.

Now it's war, he told himself. He was tempted to turn the pinto north and escape back into the mountains. Hadn't he done it before? But whatever was lost wouldn't be found in the high country. And Willie Delamer wouldn't leave Travis Cobb to face peril alone—not again!

It was nearly dusk when Willie passed Buffalo Hollow and nudged his weary mustang the final two miles to the Cobb ranch. Buzzards circled the river, looking for a twilight meal, and Willie frowned. It seemed death waited at every turn. Was there any escaping it?

It was a dusty, bedraggled Willie Delamer that finally appeared at the shed that served Travis Cobb as a barn. Only the faintest trace of the sun remained. As Willie stripped the saddle from the pinto and found the animal a bucket of water, Davy appeared.

"You look to've had a day of it," the young man observed. "I'll take your horse."

"No, it's for me to do," Willie objected. "He stood by me well today. He deserves a good rub and soft grass to nibble."

"Gus Slocum came by with the news," Davy explained as he dragged the saddle to the tack room.

"Oh?" Willie asked.

"Yeah!" Jesse added as he stepped over beside his brother. "You shot George Deaton. And Ty Phelps, too. Over a hand of cards!"

"I wasn't looking for trouble!" Willie insisted. "They come after me."

"Sure, they did. After you cheated their boss at cards, showed him up in front o' half the town. Expected him to shake your hand, I suppose."

"I didn't do anything they weren't doing," Willie argued. "And I didn't know you to be so concerned for those cowboys. Or for Romney Fairchild."

"Willie . . ." Davy whispered. But Jesse turned his brother toward the house and pushed him out of the way.

"They'll ride down here and kill us all," Jesse declared, staring at Willie with hateful eyes. "Did you have to kill his son? Lord, they say there wasn't enough face left to tell who he was."

"That sure as day wasn't my fault," Willie growled. "Was his own fool gun did it. I never fired."

"That won't be how his pa views things."

"And how would you know?"

"He paid us a visit," Jesse said, stepping closer. Now Willie could see that in addition to the bruises, Jesse had a wicked slash across one cheek. "Buggy whip does a fine job on a man, doesn't it? We got three days to sell out and get clear. Elsewise . . ."

"I'm sorry," Willie muttered, sensing the pain in the younger man's soul. "For what happened to you, I mean. As to the other, Fairchild would have come anyway. He's buying up land along the river, and he'll need a high water crossing."

"He's not the first one to want our land."

"And you don't figure he'd come except for me taking a hand of cards in Fort Griffin Town?" Willie laughed. "Jesse, he's been a long time planning this. As for the two men he lost, and the third who skedaddled, there are plenty more of that caliber to be come by."

"And his son?"

"Wasn't too busy mourning to pay you a call. Next time maybe I'll be meeting him personal."

"Yeah? Maybe you'll shoot each other and do the country a favor."

Willie recognized the pain etched on Jesse's face and left the words to roll around in the air until they died unanswered. Finally Jesse turned away, leaving Willie to work his horse in solitude. Travis appeared half an hour later with a platter of cold buffalo strips and some greens.

"Jess's had a hard time," Travis explained as he offered Willie the food. "Took Pa's dyin' personal. If he could've hit back at somebody, maybe it would've passed. As it was, the sore just festered."

"Sure," Willie muttered. "I don't take it personal. Trav, I learned a thing or two in town."

"Albany or the Flat?"

"Mostly Albany. This Fairchild fellow's put together a strip of land between the Tonkawas' camp and Ted's place. Then, too, he's bought the well-watered sections north and south. All that's left for him to put together a railroad right-of-way or a toll road's a high water crossing."

"So he'll want that from me."

"Or Ted. I don't figure him to sell. What about you?"

"I moved west once," Travis grumbled. "I never was any good at runnin' from a fight. Still, there's Irene and the little ones to consider."

"Might cost, Trav," Willie warned.

"Always has, Willie. And anyway, I figure Fairchild's already paid his share. No matter whether we sell or not, he'll want blood for blood."

"Don't they always?" Willie asked as he started on the food.

Later that night they sat on the porch and mapped strategy. It was like old times, especially when the two of them realized the long odds they faced.

"Be different if we tied in with Ted," Willie noted. "He's got two range crews."

"For now it's my fight," Travis objected. "Ain't time to call in reinforcements yet."

Willie deemed it Travis's decision to make, but he was wary nevertheless. Two peaceful days followed the death of Andrew Fairchild, though, and Lewis Slocum brought word that Fairchild and his henchmen had cleared out of the Flat.

"Maybe it's over," Travis said hopefully.

"That'd be too easy," Willie declared. "Nothing ever was that I can remember. You, Trav?"

"No," Travis confessed.

It seemed for once, though, that the storm might pass. Willie alternately busied himself cleaning and reworking pistols and rifles, working the rogue stallion at the corral, and carrying young Mike and his little brothers about on weary shoulders. The slit in Willie's side finally scarred over, and Irene's cooking drove the gaunt tinge from his face.

Even while Willie warmed with the wonderful glow cast by his new sense of belonging, he watched the distant range for buggy tracks and unknown riders. Finally they came.

He was a mile upstream of the house when the distant echo of a rifle shot fractured the morning. A second followed, as did a third. Willie froze but an instant as he studied the sounds. To the west several small creeks cut nasty ravines in the sandy terrain. Jesse and Bobby Cobb had left earlier to round up a batch of strays that had wandered out that way.

Fine place for an ambush, Willie told himself as he turned the pinto in the direction of the shooting. Now other rifles had joined the fight. Willie howled furiously and slapped the pinto into a gallop. Man and rider flew across the rugged landscape.

A wiser man might have thought things out, made a plan. Only a fool rushed headlong into a fight. But then war had always been a fool's game. For three years Willie Delamer had ridden the forests and fields of Virginia relying on instinct and nerve for survival. They stood him in good stead then, and in the ten years afterward. It was the howling gray ghost of a cavalryman who now charged through a stand of junipers, firing twin pistols and scattering three cowboys as he raced along to a boulder-strewn hollow where Jesse Cobb fought desperately to hold on.

For the first time since returning to Texas Willie saw fear in Jesse's eyes. And more. There was a trace of the boy who had once shared sunny days on the Brazos. Willie was almost to the rocks when a volley swept the slope, nicking his left boot and killing the pinto.

The horse screamed as it fell, pitching Willie forward. He only barely hung on to his pistols. The precious Winchester remained in its scabbard, buried under a mountain of bleeding horseflesh.

"Jess?" Willie called as he scrambled uphill amidst a shower of bullets.

"They're all around us!" Jesse cried. "Ten, twenty of 'em."

"I'd judge less," Willie said, reloading his pistols and staring at the trapped rifle. "You alone?"

"No," Jesse said, shaking his head. "Bobby's back there watchin' my back. And I'm watchin' his."

"I'll have a look," Willie promised as he offered a reassuring nod. "Then we'll see about slipping out of this noose."

"Yes, sir," Jesse replied, firing toward an encroaching cowboy. "I'll be here."

Willie slithered through the rocks, searching for Bobby Cobb. That stretch of the ravine was deadly silent. Jesse might not have noticed, but Willie did. It spurred him on.

Fifteen yards from where Jesse was holding off the bushwhackers, Willie detected movement. He expected Bobby's dark hair and grinning face. Instead he spied a pair of strangers climbing up the side of the slope. If they'd gotten there five minutes earlier, Willie would have been a sitting duck.

Your bad luck, Willie said as he fixed the first man in his pistol sights. The resulting blast threw the lead raider onto his companion.

"Watch where you're shootin'!" the second man shouted. "You just hit Lem!"

Willie's second shot struck as well, splintering jawbone, and sending the second ambusher writhing to the ground.

"Major, help!" Bobby Cobb called as he dragged himself behind the cover of a boulder. "They got my rifle. They—"

A fresh attack began, and Willie leveled his pistols and opened fire. The bullets, fired rapidly as they were, broke the charge and sent the four young raiders diving for shelter.

"Here," Willie said, prying a Winchester from the lifeless hands of the first bushwhacker. As Willie handed over the weapon, he observed blood running down Bobby's left arm.

"You're hurt," Willie observed. "Bad?"

"Bad enough," Bobby said, accepting the rifle. "Just above the left elbow."

Willie scowled as he examined the wound. The bullet had passed through the meat of the arm, though, and it was a simple matter to bind the wound and put a halt to the bleeding.

"Figure I'll live?" Bobby asked, wincing when Willie tightened the binding.

"Expect so," Willie declared. "Cobbs are generally too stringy and mule-backed to let any one bullet do 'em much harm."

"Could be others comin' along," Bobby pointed out.

"No, it's these other folks' turn to get shot up."

"I can hold 'em a bit," Bobby said as he steadied his rifle. "Maybe you should have a look at Jess."

"He's fine," Willie assured the young man. "They'll come this way, I expect. Jess's got himself rocked in on three sides. No way up there that won't sting 'em good. On the other hand, he's got a blind spot to his back."

"No, we're here," Bobby boasted.

"Sure, we are," Willie agreed. He matched Bobby's contagious grin and looked over the ground before them. "Not many ways to get at us. I'd guess it'll be one big charge. They'll count on the fire to keep our heads down. If we make 'em pay, they'll scatter sure."

"Sounds right by me," Bobby said, concentrating on the rocky slope. "Wouldn't mind payin' 'em for my arm."

As Willie predicted, the raiders reformed. One raced out and dragged his wounded comrade to cover. Willie motioned Bobby to let it pass. Better to await the charge. And the time was put to better use reloading.

"Hey, you up there!" a familiar voice suddenly called. Willie glanced over the boulder and found Leon Martley rising. "It's near over, you know. Best give it up. All we want's to take you in, hold you hostage against your brother signin' over a deed. Nothin' worth dyin', you see. You got years o' high livin' ahead o' you."

"Devil take you!" Bobby shouted, firing a bullet past Martley's ear.

"Let's go, men!" Martley shouted, and five men started up the slope. Bobby opened up on them, and three immediately fled. Martley and one other man continued. Willie steadied his aim and hit both. Martley clutched a shattered knee, and his companion grabbed a right arm near severed at the elbow.

"Come on!" Bobby urged. "Well?"

"Be another day!" Martley swore as he limped to cover.

"For some!" Bobby called. "Not for all."

Willie nodded his agreement. The stiffening body to their left attested to the fact. As for the other raiders, they collected after a fashion and got mounted.

"One or two might be in range," Bobby observed. "My rifle could just—"

"Stay put," Willie urged. "They got rifles, too, and one or two could be pointed up here even now. Let 'em go and nurse their wounds. Some are sure to leave. A man like Fairchild won't hold men, not once the blood's flowing. Money's got to get better for a man to risk his hide."

"I'd say so," Jesse remarked as he crawled over. "Little brother, you got yourself shot!"

"Not too bad," Willie pointed out. "Figure you can find some horses? Mine's lying dead back there."

"I tied our ponies yonder by the spring," Bobby explained. "Bet them bushwhackers left a mount or two below."

"I'll have a look," Jesse said, setting off. He returned ten minutes later with three animals. Willie's saddle and rifle were atop a tall roan mare.

"Not altogether a bad horse," Jesse said as he dropped the reins at Willie's side. "Recognize the brand?"

"Jess, he come to help!" Bobby barked.

"There's time to argue later," Willie added as he helped Bobby rise. "We've got a wounded man to get home."

"What'll I tell Trav?" Jesse suddenly gasped. "I was oldest. Was my job to look after him."

"Isn't your fault," Willie said as he boosted Bobby up onto his horse. "There'll come a reckoning, Bobby," he added. "I promise you that!"

"Ain't your fault, either," Jesse said, extending a trembling hand toward Willie.

"Doesn't sound like you, Jess," Willie said as he met the hand with his own. The grip was firm, ironlike.

"If you hadn't come, we'd both be dead," Jesse replied. "Hate to admit it, but there it is."

"You had a good position. No, you'd done all right."

"You picked up that lyin' habit off your brother, I'm guessin'," Jesse said, trying unsuccessfully to manage a smile. "Trav told me plenty o' times how you helped, but I only remember Pa's broken heart."

"It's a hard thing, losing a father," Willie observed. "Lost mine, too. And many a good friend since."

"Does it get easier after a time?"

"No," Willie said, shuddering as he released his hold on Jesse's hand. "Just hollows out a little more of what you thought was your heart."

"You two plannin' to jaw away the rest o' the day?" Bobby asked impatiently. "Them others might not stay away forever, you know."

"He's got a point," Jesse confessed.

"Then lead away," Willie suggested.

Jesse turned his horse homeward, and the three of them cautiously made their way to the river and along to the house. Travis met them halfway, his face pale with concern.

"Wasn't much of a fight once the Major happened by," Bobby declared. "Come chargin' down on them bushwhackers, pistols blazin', and sent 'em hightailin'!"

"Was enough of a fight you got shot," Jesse declared. "Sorry, Trav. I should've seen it comin'. There were tracks around, and I . . ."

"You got through it," Travis argued. "That's the only thing that really matters in a fight. Now let's get home before fresh trouble happens along."

Jesse allowed Travis to take the lead, and the four of them nudged their ponies into a trot. In no time at all they were back at the house. Jesse took charge of the animals, and Willie helped Bobby into the kitchen.

"Leave him to me," Irene announced as she located a washbasin. "I haven't done any real cutting on a man since the war."

"Bullet passed through," Bobby explained. "No cuttin' to do."

"Bullets leave fragments," she grumbled. "You leave the doctor to her business, won't you. As for the rest of you, off!" she added, waving Mike, Josh, and Art from the room. Willie frowned.

"Did you sting 'em some?" Travis asked when they sat together on the porch.

"A bit," Willie answered. "Killed one for certain, and I think I spied another body, likely dropped by Jesse. Couple wounded, too."

"That'll give 'em cause to think it out," Travis said, nodding to himself. "Fairchild might just decide the price's past payin'."

"I hope so," Willie said, resting his head against the oak picket wall of the house. "But I wouldn't wager more'n a dollar on it."

"Stakes're higher in this game, old friend."

"Sure they are," Willie agreed. "Life and death."

CHAPTER 11

Life had a way of turning things upside down. Willie was sitting on the porch, whittling a horse out of a piece of cedar, when he heard a horse approaching. Instantly he set aside the wood, returned his knife to the scabbard on his boot, and set out to investigate. Travis and Jesse appeared as well. The three of them stood there, guns drawn and frowning heavily, when a slender dark-haired boy of twelve or so galloped up the trail.

"Whoa," the boy called, reining his horse to a stop. "Mr. Cobb?"

Travis laughed.

"Tim, whatever's brought you racin' out here so late in the evenin'?" Travis asked as he lowered his rifle. "Too late for ridin' surely, and you have a hard trip back to Albany."

"Didn't come to ride," the boy explained. "Somebody sent me."

"Somebody?" Willie asked. "Who?"

"One of 'em's named Martley," the boy explained. "Others I don't know. Save for the buggy-whip fellow. He brought some papers to the jailhouse a week or so ago. I recall Grandpa didn't find much use for him. Beat his horses."

"Your name'd be Little then," Willie remarked.

"That's me," Tim said, stretching himself a bit. "Little

Tim, or Tim Little. One's the same as t'other, Grandpa tells me."

"I had a talk with your grandpa," Willie said, noticing the boy's momentary grin fade to a sour frown. "Frank's pa, Trav."

"I know Mr. Little," Travis explained. "Tim too. He comes out here to haunt the range. Figures to steal workin' boys from their chores. Only not this time, huh, Tim?"

"Well, sir, I did come ridin'," Tim replied. "With Lewis and Lamar. Only we were down by the river, and these fellows come on us sudden, wavin' guns and hollerin'."

"And the others?" Willie asked.

"Martley and the buggy-whip man took 'em. Said to go fetch their pa. Mr. Cobb, I mean. They think they got Mike, I guess. I don't think they'd hurt 'em."

"Have you been to the Slocum place?" Travis asked.

"I was scared to," Tim confessed. He shuddered, and Willie pulled the boy off his horse. The animal and the boy were both lathered from hard riding. "You're Major Delamer, ain't you?" Tim asked. "Grandpa says you're a man to put things right. That buggy-whip man's talkin' crazy, Major. Said Mr. Cobb rides up there alone and signs over his ranch, or else . . ."

"Else what?" Jesse asked angrily.

"Says he'll cut off their ears," Tim explained with wide eyes. "First day one ear. Second two."

"And then?" Travis asked.

"He wouldn't tell me," Tim answered. "I don't know. Maybe fingers. He looked like he'd do it, Mr. Cobb."

"Jesse, ride out and tell Ted Slocum," Travis instructed.

"You can't," Tim said. "Don't you see? They followed me. If they think you're goin' for help, they'll start on them ears now."

"I won't give up the ranch," Travis vowed.

"No, you won't," Willie agreed. "It's for Tim to ride to Ted's place and let him know what's about. Trav, you and Jesse meet me at the river."

"What'll you do?" Travis asked.

"Do some following of my own," Willie explained. "Tim, you think you're up to riding a bit more?"

"If I had a fresh mount," the boy said, staring at the corral. "The one that's trailin' me's ridin' a brown horse with white speckles, Major. Ain't hard to see him."

"No, I expect not," Willie said, smiling grimly.

With Jesse's help, Willie managed to throw Tim's saddle on a fresh pony and prepare a roan stallion for himself. After stuffing Tim with cold beef and biscuits and half drowning him with milk, Irene Cobb agreed the boy should go. Willie, meanwhile, had led his horse around behind the shed and ridden down a ravine. He waited there while Tim started out toward the Slocum ranch. Sure enough, the trailing rider followed. Willie had no trouble falling in behind him and laying the barrel of his Winchester across the villain's head.

"You got him good, Major!" Tim howled.

"Never you mind that," Willie said. "Ride and tell Ted what's happened. Can you lead them to where Fairchild's holding the boys?"

"Who?" Tim asked.

"The buggy-whip man. And Martley. You remember where they were?"

"Yes, sir, Major. I'll bring 'em along fast as I can."

"Hurry," Willie urged. After all, three men wouldn't stack up well against Fairchild's outfit.

After tying the unconscious Fairchild man to a handy live oak, Willie set off for the river. He met Travis and Jesse there, as planned. The two Cobbs were armed to the teeth and angry to boot. It was bad enough that Bobby and Jesse had been ambushed. Threatening harm to the Slocum boys had set blood to boiling.

"Best calm down," Willie warned. "This is a moment for cool heads. Charging in there yelling bloody murder's sure to get Lewis and Lamar killed."

"Only know one fellow who rides around hollerin' and shootin' off pistols," Jesse replied. "So, how's it to be done?"

"Remember that time north of Falmouth?" Willie asked

Travis. "When we snatched that Louisiana colonel from the Yanks?"

"I do," Travis said, grinning. "You don't mean to do all of it, though. Not with the three of us."

"Won't be enough to snatch back the boys," Willie said, frowning heavily. "Got to get Fairchild's attention. And show him up for what he is."

"What do you mean to do?" Jesse asked.

"You'll see," Travis said, grinning. "If we can pull it off, that is."

"We will," Willie assured his companions. "Have faith."

They backtracked their way close to three miles before locating Fairchild's camp. He had a pair of tents set up on the north bank of the river. Three men sat around a small campfire. A fourth kept watch outside the right-hand tent. Fairchild and Martley were ten yards away, talking. The seventh and eighth men kept watch on either side of the river.

"I'll take the one on the north bank," Willie announced. "Give me ten minutes afterward to get the boys clear. Then you take the guard on this bank and be ready to open up on the camp. Understand?"

"I understand even then they'll have us outnumbered two to one," Jesse protested.

"They won't know that," Willie declared, grinning. "Believe me. They'll think a regiment of cavalry's come calling."

Jesse remained doubtful, but Travis led his brother along. Willie dismounted, tied off his horse, and walked downstream a ways. He then splashed across the river, taking care to keep the long-barreled Winchester and his twin Colts dry. Finally he wove his way through tall grass to where a stand of willows bounded Fairchild's camp.

The guard strolled lazily nearby. Then he suddenly rested his rifle against the trunk of a willow and slipped over into the tall grass. Willie couldn't help grinning as the guard dug a shallow hole in the ground with the heel of his boot and began loosening his trousers. Willie slung the Winchester like a club and bashed the fool guard across his forehead.

The guard fell back in a heap, and Willie quickly disarmed him.

The next step was trickier. Willie collected the guard's rifle and crawled over to the tents. They were identical, and one was sure to contain the young Slocums. Which one, though? And what was in the other? It might well house a dozen Fairchild hands, each one armed and ready. Willie doubted that, though. There was the guard watching the door of the nearest shelter, too, so Willie drew out his knife and slashed the back side of that tent.

Inside Lewis and Lamar gazed in amazement as Willie crept over. Willie motioned for silence as he cut their ropes.

"Now, follow me," he whispered.

The two boys snaked after Willie, and he in turn led them past the willows to a rocky ravine.

"Take the rifles," Willie advised. "Wait here. Tim Little's gone to fetch your papa, and the Cobb boys are across the river. Leave us to handle the rest."

"But . . . how?" Lewis cried.

"They were about to cut my ears off," Lamar added. "That fellow Fairchild already had a go at Lewis."

Willie gazed angrily as Lewis bared his chest. Whip marks showed up like white slashes on the youngster's leathery hide.

"Wait here," Willie repeated.

"Not on your life," Lamar objected. "We can both shoot just fine. And we got more reason'n anybody to be in on this fight."

"Don't expect it to come to a fight," Willie told them. They nevertheless refused to stay behind, and Willie found himself leading the way back to the willows. He'd only been there a matter of seconds when the guard on the far side of the river cried out.

"Horses!" he screamed.

Jesse Cobb fired a single bullet through the guard's head, and the man collapsed in a heap.

"Grab your rifles!" Fairchild ordered.

Willie fired twice at the stacked weapons, and the men gazed nervously around.

"Stay put!" Willie shouted.

The gunman keeping watch on the tent ducked inside, discovered the hostages gone, and reported the news to Fairchild.

"That can't be!" the Englishman yelled.

The guard made a move toward the rifles then, and Lamar Slocum coldly cut him down.

"Well, Fairchild?" Willie called. "Five left. Care to press your luck?"

"I'm unarmed!" Fairchild claimed. "I'm not resisting. Clearly, shooting me would be murder."

"And what was it when you and your men shot Bobby?" Travis hollered. "Well?"

"That was the Cobb boy? We meant only to scare them," Fairchild pleaded. "You must see that. It's the land at issue. Not lives."

"You're wrong!" Ted Slocum shouted as he rode up with a dozen men. "Any man threatens my boys is a corpse!"

"No, Ted," Willie called as Slocum aimed a pistol at Fairchild's head.

"We got a plan, Ted," Travis added. "Remember the Falmouth raid? That Yank general and his fancy drawers!"

"Lord, I do," Slocum said, fighting unsuccessfully to keep a straight face. "You don't mean to . . ."

"Bet he's got a trunk full o' silk drawers," Travis said, splashing over to the second tent and tearing his way inside. He dragged out a trunk and began tossing clothes here and there.

"Mind those things!" Fairchild shouted. "That's a two-hundred-dollar coat there!"

"Not anymore," Lamar said, trotting over and rending the garment in two.

"Jesse, why don't you see these other fellows get cared for?" Willie asked, and Jesse motioned for Gus Slocum and a half-dozen others to help tend the captives. The TS hands collected gunbelts and weapons.

"No, not yet," Travis said when Jesse began binding Martley's wrists with canvas strips torn from the tent. "Wouldn't want these poor fellows passin' out from the heat. Strip down to your personals, gents," Travis instructed. "Boots too,

Leon. Gus, don't you figure that fire's burnin' kind o' low. See anything here that'd burn?''

"Yes, sir!" Gus said, waving his younger brothers toward the garments the raiders were reluctantly discarding. Soon smoke spiraled skyward from flaming boots and stockings, shirts and trousers. As for Fairchild, the rotund Englishman stood bare to the waist in his silk drawers while Willie poured molasses over his bare feet and legs.

"Texas ants are partial to the flavor," Willie explained. "I expect you'll have a time getting acquainted with 'em on your way to town."

"Isn't it enough that you've murdered my son?" Fairchild sobbed. "You've murdered good men."

"No, that's been altogether your own doing," Willie said. He spotted the buggy whip then and touched the tip of the wicked strap to the Englishman's nose. "I know you, Fairchild. You're the worst sort of man. You've hidden behind others all your life. Lord knows what brought you to this country. Likely your native land's tossed you to the rats!

"I don't know why you came here. I don't care. I want you gone. Elsewise when we meet next, I'll be the one carving ears. Understand?"

"Yes, I do understand," Fairchild replied. "You needn't subject me to such humiliation, however."

"Needn't I?" Willie asked mockingly. "Well, I'll leave that to the injured party. How 'bout it, Lewis?"

"I'd roll him down a cactus-covered hillside," Lewis said, opening his shirt for his father to view. Ted's face paled, and his fiery eyes glared at Fairchild.

"This ain't enough," Slocum declared. "Not for a man whips boys!"

"Set him afire!" one of the cowboys suggested. "Let's roast ourselves a varmint. Comanche-style."

Fairchild gazed in horror as Ted Slocum held a branch to the fire and raised the flaming torch.

"No, I beg of you," Fairchild pleaded, dropping to his knees. "God have mercy upon me. I only intended to frighten them."

"He shot Bobby," Jesse pointed out.

93

"Just take him to town," Willie argued. "It'll be enough."

"Will it?" Slocum asked as he carried the burning branch over and held it near Fairchild's face. "Well? Will we ever see you in these parts again, mister?"

"Never!" Fairchild screamed.

"If we do, you know what awaits you," Travis warned. Slocum then tossed his branch onto the buggy and watched the vehicle burn. Jesse and Gus assembled the Fairchild horses and sent them stampeding down the river.

"Now, it's time you boys took a walk to Fort Griffin," Slocum announced. "Fairchild, best you lead the way."

"We can't walk all that way with no boots," Martley grumbled. "I've just had a bullet cut from my leg!"

"Well, it's your choice," Jesse said, firing a pistol at the gunman's toes.

"All right! I'll walk," Martley howled. "Only we'll be settlin' accounts one day."

"Care to do it now?" Willie asked.

"Got some walkin' to do now," Martley muttered. "Be later, I'm guessin'."

"Will it?" Gus asked, laughing.

Fairchild then led his half-naked procession off along the river toward Fort Griffin. Willie listened to the cowboys taunting the captured raiders. It would take a lot of nerve for any one of them to show his face in Shackleford County thereafter. The dizzy guard and the captured tracker were turned over to Jesse, who agreed to conduct them to the sheriff in Albany.

"I guess we turned the tables on 'em, all right," Travis boasted as he and Willie splashed back across the Clear Fork.

"Did a fair job of it, I'd say," Willie agreed. "Now we wait and see if the lesson takes."

CHAPTER 12

In a week's time Romney Fairchild was the laughingstock of western Texas. The mere mention of the Englishman brought hoots and jests. More to the point, his hirelings deserted him in pairs. By mid-September only Leon Martley remained.

"He's finished," Ted Slocum declared. "Men'll take risks to earn a few dollars, but they won't have themselves laughed at. Sendin' that snake into town in his drawers was genius. Why, I heard Miss Myra's gals've started callin' him 'Useless.' "

Willie was glad to see his friend cheered so, and he wanted to believe it, too. Fairchild never ventured past the Flat, after all, and soon he boarded a northbound stagecoach and vanished altogether. Still, Willie had a sixth sense about trouble, and he wasn't convinced the final page of that story had been turned.

"If he's got any sense, he's gone," Elvira Slocum grumbled angrily. "It's for certain the decent people of Shackleford County won't tolerate a kidnapper or a murderer!"

"Nor a cardsharp, either," Gus added. "Didn't find himself much cheered in the gaming houses at the Flat, and they don't turn many away."

"If we had even a little law, we'd see Fairchild hung," Elvira pointed out. "That Nathan Pennypacker calls himself sheriff, but he didn't even bother to hold those gunmen Jesse turned over to him.''

"They weren't much of a threat, senseless as they were," Gus observed. "No point to feedin' 'em at county expense while they mend their hurts.''

"Should've shot the whole bunch when we had the chance," a still-shaken Lewis asserted.

"Lew?" Willie asked.

"You didn't see 'em holdin' that knife to us," Lamar explained. "Ain't any forgettin' nor forgivin' such a thing.''

Willie guessed not. And he grieved that Lewis and Lamar should have become so hard-hearted.

The onset of autumn brought no relief from the searing heat. Not so much as a drop of rain fell. The creeks and pools that normally dotted the landscape shrank daily until finally only the river remained wet.

"Leastwise we're not farmers," Travis noted. "We can move stock to the river. Cornstalks just wither and die.''

But moving ten thousand longhorn cattle was no easy feat. Between the TS Ranch and Travis's smaller place there were nearly that many animals. A good third of them were now stranded on the fringes of the range and wanted rounding up and driving to the water.

"No point to cursin' luck," Travis told his brothers. "Best to get right after it.''

"At least there's no brandin' to do," Bobby said, slipping his wounded arm in a sling. "Truth is, I been lyin' 'round so much lately I welcome the work.''

"Well, not everybody's had it so soft," Jesse complained. "Now, after eatin' dust all the way to Kansas in the spring, we end up doin' it again in September. Don't the fool clouds know to bring rain?''

"Don't know," Travis confessed. "Don't think I've seen a cloud since midsummer.''

Neither had Willie. The Texas plain was such a contrast to the rainy slopes of the Rockies. But Travis was right. There wasn't much gained by grumbling. And there were plenty of jobs to occupy a man's attention.

They started early. To begin with, Travis and his brothers combed the far eastern range, driving strays down a dozen ravines toward the river. Willie, together with Lewis and Lamar Slocum, and aided by three TS hands, combed the hills that formed the southern boundary of both ranches, urging the small collections of cattle they came across north to the winding river. It was hot, dusty work, and it left them cross and exhausted at day's end.

"Maybe bein' tied up in that tent wasn't such a bad fate after all," Lewis remarked after three days of prowling the range.

"Sure," Willie said, grinning. "What's an ear or two?"

For the first time in weeks Lewis managed to laugh. It was a sign of healing, Willie thought.

He was glad, for there was little time to look after the young Slocums. If chasing reluctant longhorns out of every hollow and thicket south of the Clear Fork wasn't enough to vex a man's soul, Willie had the second chore of breaking in a new horse. The pinto wasn't a cow pony, of course, and Willie would surely have found himself atop another animal anyway. But when Travis offered a choice of mounts in recompense for the fallen pinto, Willie immediately selected Stinger.

"Can't mean it!" Bobby howled. "That horse's meaner'n sin, Major. It likes to hurt people."

Even Jesse warned of danger.

"A man'd have to be missin' some o' his senses to sit that horse without a lot o' money on the line," Jesse declared. "I've near fed that devil to the buzzards a dozen times."

"Leave him to me," Willie told them. "It's just a matter of getting ourselves acquainted." But although Stinger accepted a saddle now, the animal continued his ill-tempered ways. Just when Willie relaxed, the mustang would turn to thrashing and bucking. Most times Willie stayed mounted, but four or five times he'd flown off into the brush, delighting his young companions.

Stinger never bolted afterward. The horse just gazed down at its would-be rider with a sort of bemused snarl.

"I'd get myself another horse," Ted Slocum advised when

97

the southern range had finally been swept clear of strays. "I've got a dozen good saddle ponies you can choose from."

"No, thanks," Willie replied. "We're a pair, I figure. Neither one of us's exactly fit for civilized company. But we suit each other well enough."

It was one truth Willie had discovered. The second was that hard as working cattle was, it took him back to a world he'd left long ago. And if it was impossible to consider whipping steers down ravines or coaxing a bull out of a mud wallow peaceful work, at least it could be done without powder and lead—and death.

The best parts of those days were their aftermath. Toward dusk the cowboys would collect at the river to wash off the dust and exhaustion. Mike Cobb and his brothers, together with Albany strays like Tim Little, would join them, and amid the pranks and water fights the weariness flowed from a man like so much accumulated sweat.

"Anybody ever see a boy with such a white bottom?" Lamar cried one afternoon when Tim raced by, chasing Josh through the shallows.

"It's amazin' what town livin'll do to you," Lewis added.

Little Tim took immediate offense, but the twelve-year-old was no match for the older boys, and he only barely escaped a branding.

"Did you ever see such a collection o' mischief?" Travis asked Willie. "Nothin' but skin, bone, hair, and devilment."

"Were we any different?" Willie asked.

"Mind you don't tell them," Travis said, grinning. "They think old men like ourselves were born leathery hard and scarred up. Be a disappointment to learn otherwise."

"I suppose," Willie confessed. "Must be a comfort to see yourself reborn in those boys."

"Is," Travis agreed. "You ought to get yourself a few, Willie. Take the edge off some o' the disappointments."

"Such as?"

"Losin' Pa. And the old place. Now we've got the cattle off the south range, you might take a few days, ride out to the cliffs, maybe swim over and visit your ma and pa."

"The ranch, you mean?"

"Chase off some ghosts. Didn't you say it yourself? You come back to find somethin' left behind."

"Yes, and I thought it was there on the river where we swam away a dozen summers. I figured to climb the high places where Yellow Shirt taught me the buffalo prayers, where we laid Red Wolf to rest with the spirits of his people. I was wrong, though. What I really missed is right here."

"What's that, old friend?"

"Purpose," Willie said, eyeing Hood and Hill Slocum wrestling nearby. "Belonging."

"And here I thought it was mostly noise," Travis said, laughing.

"Noise is rare precious sometimes," Willie explained. "You remember how quiet the nights were at Petersburg. Shoot, somebody'd strike up a song, and two armies'd cheer. I still hear that Irish tenor singing his ballads. I didn't understand half the words, but the tune was enough to melt your heart. Silence has a cruel edge, Trav."

"Stay a bit," Travis said, resting a weary hand on Willie's shoulder. "Ain't much of it to be found hereabouts."

They were thereupon attacked by a small army of half-grown savages and dragged into the river. There, amid cackling children and grazing cattle, Willie finally felt as if he'd gotten home.

The storm came after breakfast that next morning. At first Willie stared at the wall of gray-black clouds and thought he was viewing a mirage. The air suddenly turned cold, though, and a hush fell upon the land.

"Lord help us," Willie said, staring at the smoky lines that told where rain was falling to the north.

"Can't you remember what rain looks like, Willie?" Bobby asked as he stepped outside. "Look there. It's wet on the Red River, I'll bet. We'll get some water back on that south range. Figures, now we've moved the stock."

"You got a cellar?" Willie suddenly asked.

"Cellar?" Bobby cried. "Ever dig holes for corral posts in this country? Solid rock six inches down."

"Where do you go to cover?" Willie asked, his forehead etched with deep furrows.

"Cover?" Bobby asked, not understanding. "The house, I suppose."

"You won't have a house an hour from now," Willie declared. "Better get your family out and find a ravine that'll offer some cover."

"You crazy?"

"No," Willie said, trotting to the corral and sliding back rails so the horses could escape. Even the gentlest of the animals hurried off, whining the alarm.

"Willie, you gone crazy?" Travis asked as he raced out the door.

"Look!" Willie said, pointing to a dark wall of swirling cloud that seemed to boil down toward them.

"Be some wind comin'," Travis announced.

"More'n that house'll take," Willie pointed out. "Or the shed."

"There's cover a hundred yards west. A ravine crowned with rock."

"Stay out of the stream bed," Willie warned. "It could flood."

"Will," Travis said, paling. "Mike and Tim Little passed the night with the Slocum boys down on the river. Right on the shore."

"Ain't a one of 'em's seen a twister before," Bobby said as he stared at the wicked tail that suddenly dipped out of the cloud. "Best I go get 'em."

"You get that arm to cover," Willie advised. "I'll get the boys."

"That's my job," Travis argued.

"You got a wife and little ones here," Willie said, locating Stinger pawing the sandy ground a hundred feet away. "Anyway, I've got a horse yonder, and the other mounts are scattered far and wide. Leave it to me and ole Stinger. We'll get 'em to cover."

"Cover?" Bobby called. "What cover?"

"Leave it to me," Willie repeated as he dashed toward the anxious mustang. "I'll find some."

100

Willie climbed onto Stinger's bare back and urged the horse into a gallop. The animal seemed to be waiting for the command, for its feet instantly took flight, and Willie was racing along the river like winged fury. He covered the mile and a quarter to the boys' camp while the darkening sky came earthward. Already Willie detected the clattering sound of the twister. Once he'd slept beside the Union Pacific tracks in Kansas. Twenty cattle cars rumbled past a hair after midnight, shaking Willie from his bed. The sound was the same, and the ground trembled to its tempo.

"Major?" Lewis Slocum cried as Willie leaped off Stinger and rushed toward where the boys had collected around the cook fire. He grabbed Hood with one arm, picked up little Hill in the other and urged the older boys to follow.

"Sir?" Tim Little asked. "Where are we goin'?"

"Anywhere!" Mike Cobb yelled. "The sky's fallin' on top o' us here."

"It's a twister!" Lamar yelled.

The others stared but a second at the spiral of black fury carving up the range beyond the river. Then they grabbed their belongings and followed Willie past a line of willows and along toward a boulder-strewn slope.

"Stay off the crown," Willie advised. "There, along that rock wall. Get low and cover your heads. Now!"

Willie flew that way in spite of the weight of the young Slocums. He managed to locate a sizable boulder and nestle Hood and Hill in a sort of hollow.

"The rest of you dig yourselves in!" Willie shouted over the rumbling of the cyclone. He felt the cold touch of the wind, was slapped by flaying rain and pelted by hail. He felt none of it. His sole thought was to cover the children.

At the same time he felt the warm touch of the others beside him and he heard Lamar's reassuring calm offered the younger boys. The storm suddenly swallowed those words as it churned along the river, uprooting trees as a man might pluck tomato plants. Rocks flew. Branches and boards ricocheted off the protective wall of rock. Willie heard the faint whine of a horse and worried over Stinger. Then, as the thundering tempest hurled past, the boys gazed up in wonder.

"There's a longhorn flyin' by!" Lewis shouted in disbelief.

"Look there!" Hood howled, pointing to boards flung beside the river. "Those're from our house!"

"Can't a storm come from two directions at once," Mike argued.

"This one can," Willie said, staring wide-eyed at a swath of destruction a hundred feet wide torn across the rolling range. He inspected the youngsters next. Lewis had a few scratches courtesy of a flying mesquite limb, and everyone had a knot or two raised by a hailstone. The ground was littered with them, and Tim located two the size of an eyeball.

"Regular eyeball, you mean," Willie said, shaking off the anxiety brought by the storm. "Mine were double when they saw that devil's tail."

"Devil's tail?" Mike asked. "Was a twister."

"Same thing," Willie said, motioning his soggy companions closer. "But I think maybe the Comanches had it right when they said it was the tail of the devil. See, mostly that ole devil keeps to himself. Oh, he throws a flood or a drought at you, sure enough, but he mostly turns himself into a cougar or a wolf when he takes it into his head to torment human beings. But when he's in a real rotten humor, he goes flying around the sky, screaming and bellowing."

"And his tail?" Lewis asked, grinning.

"Comes down to churn up the earth. Just like it did today. Must've been particular set on pranking you boys. Look what it did to your camp!"

The boys turned and gazed in shock at three large trees that lay across the ashes of their fire. Rocks and debris lay everywhere. Hood and Hill's blankets were mere shreds.

"Good thing you know 'bout devil's tails, Major," Lamar said, swallowing hard. "I'm thinkin' you saved us a second time."

"Me too," Lewis said, leaning against Willie's weary side.

"Guess it's becoming a habit," Willie replied. "And I'd judge you two did your share looking after the others."

"We'd never left the camp, though," Lamar confessed. "I'll know better from now on. You can bet on that."

"That's all you can do," Willie said, nodding somberly. "Learn when life offers the chance. Now, I don't know about you youngsters, but I'm getting tired of all this rain on my head. Let's have a look back at the Cobb place and see if there's any roof left to duck under."

"I figure we ought to head home, Major," Lamar argued.

"Long walk," Willie pointed out. "And those clouds haven't gone anywhere."

"Could be we're needed," Lewis explained.

"Well, it's more likely Ted's got hands to spare for helping others, but your folks'll certainly be anxious over you. Maybe it'd be best if you went along home."

"Thanks again, Major," Lamar said as he took charge of Hood and Hill. The other Slocums echoed the sentiment, and Willie waved them good-bye. He then turned east through the ravaged countryside. Mike and Tim followed.

CHAPTER 13

Willie and his two young companions had walked only a quarter of a mile when Stinger appeared. The horse snorted a greeting, and Willie trotted over and stroked the animal's nose.

"Feel up to a ride, horse?" Willie asked.

The horse was a bit skittish, but Willie nevertheless managed to steady it enough to get mounted.

"Come on, boys," Willie called, extending a hand. "Ole Sting here's up to another passenger, or even two."

"Thanks just the same," Mike replied. "I know this horse. He don't like boys. In fact, he don't like *anybody*!"

Tim also declined the offer, and Willie found himself riding escort for the youngsters. It wasn't far, though, and what with the rain peppering them unceasingly, the boys kept up with Stinger's anxious gait.

"Not much farther," Mike announced as he splashed his way up a hillside. Tim raced along after his friend, and Willie nudged Stinger into a trot. All three of them halted when they reached the crest of the hill.

"What . . ." Mike began, sinking to his knees. Willie saw why. The cyclone had surged across the ranch buildings. The twin chimneys of the house were flat, and the plank walls had been broken and scattered over half a mile. The shed

104

had simply vanished. Even the rails of the corral were gone. The bare posts remained to haunt the scene.

"Ma? Pa?" Mike called out.

"It's all right," Willie said, climbing off his horse. "They'll have gone to cover."

"But . . ." Mike started to object. Then he saw his mother emerge from behind a pair of uprooted junipers. Instantly the thirteen-year-old dashed down the hill, and Willie noted with satisfaction that the other Cobbs rushed to meet the boy.

"They look pretty happy," Tim Little said, shaking his head. "Grandpa'd be throwin' a fit if some devil's tail went and tore his house down."

"Be madder if something happened to you, I'll wager," Willie responded. "Hard to grow a new boy. Putting up another cabin, or a barn either, isn't so big a problem."

Those words proved prophetic. Within the hour Ted Slocum rode over to have a look at the damage, and by late afternoon a dozen pairs of hands were hacking oak and juniper logs into pickets and clearing away fragments of glass, splintered planks, and damaged branches.

The Slocum place hadn't escaped harm itself. The house had gotten off lightly. Only a pair of windows had been broken, and shingles were torn from the roof. The barn had lost one wall and most of the roof. The storm had also killed twenty head of cattle and a pair of horses.

"The little ones got through fine, thanks to you, Willie," Slocum said as the two old friends walked along the river. "It seems to me like you've taken root hereabouts. Lewis got to thinkin' how with you havin' no kids of your own, maybe we ought to adopt you as sort of an uncle. I told 'em you've got nephews, but Lamar figures Sam's brood hardly counts as human bein's."

"Davy Cobb says they're good boys," Willie objected.

"He ain't known 'em in a while," Slocum replied. "And you wouldn't even recognize 'em in a gaggle. Well, would you consent to becomin' Uncle Wil? Eh?"

"Don't see there'd be any harm to it."

"Then it's settled. First chore you get, Uncle Wil, is to come stay with us till Trav gets this place rebuilt. Won't be a week 'fore they get the house up, but the shed'll wait, I figure. I'll expect you to earn your keep, o' course. The crew brought in seven range ponies that're sure to need a firm hand. Gus'll want to test himself against the meanest, and Lamar's sure to press his case. That means Lewis'll do the same. They wouldn't fight off a hint or two. I never knew a man to know horses like you.''

''I'll happily accept the invite and the job, Ted,'' Willie said, nodding. ''I'll want some time to help Trav, too, though.''

''Whole county's sure to be out here Saturday,'' Slocum explained. ''Elvira's already sent the word. We'll have a barbecue and a roof-raisin' followed by a dance. Be a fine time. Give you a chance to meet some o' the neighbors, far-off though they be. Widow Bannion's sure to come. She's a looker, and she has a nice place out toward Albany.''

''I'm not much on dancing,'' Willie argued.

''You ain't seen Rose Bannion. Nor tasted her cookin'. Red hair mixes just fine with chicken 'n dumplin's.''

Willie laughed it off. As the days passed working the Slocums mustangs into saddle ponies and cutting planks for the barn Travis planned to replace his old shed, Willie gave no thought to the barbecue or the barn dance. Not so his guests. Elvira Slocum never neglected a chance to describe one dance or another at mealtime. And whenever she managed to lead Willie off to one side, which was once or twice each day, she talked up one friend or another.

''Now you take Emma Potter,'' Elvira began after breakfast Friday. ''She's a hair older maybe, but she's got two stout boys to help work the farm. I'd guess she's got some childbearin' years left to her.''

''Does she?'' Willie asked, attempting escape.

''Well, I'll admit five boys and a girl'd be a full litter for some, Willie, but she comes of good Irish stock. I heard her own mother birthed sixteen and lost just one to fever.''

''So that would leave me ten,'' Willie said, fighting the urge to laugh.

''Eight would be more likely, as Emma's lost a year or so to widowhood.''

"If she has, it's all she's lost," Lamar said, sticking his head out the window. "Weighs more'n your horse, Uncle Wil. Two-eighty easy."

"That would seem a handful," Willie confessed.

"You mind you don't lose that waggin' tongue, Lamar Slocum!" Elvira warned. "Actually, if you don't object to skinny women, Rose Bannion's sure to come to the dance. She's a good woman, lauded by all for her keepin' of the commandments. Lost her man on the trail to Kansas."

"He drowned crossin' Red River!" Lamar called. "Bad luck. Miz Bannion's a looker."

"It's the Lord's own truth," Elvira said, blushing.

"Got a good farm, too," Lamar added.

"Yes, that's true," Elvira said, waving Lamar off with her hand. "She's had men aplenty buzzin' past her door, but she's got an independent streak. Has two pretty girls. Twelve and ten years, they are. A boy, too. Hair older'n Hood."

"And she's pretty," Lamar reminded his mother. "Real pretty. Cooks the best pie . . . next to Ma, o' course, in the county."

"Get yourself along to work, Lamar!" Elvira scolded, running him out of the house. "I'll tell Rose you'd enjoy her company for a dance or two. Shall I?"

"I'd rather you not," Willie answered. "I'm not much on dancing. Likely I'll pass the time down by the river."

"You will not, Willie Delamer," Elvira chided him. "Do you know why we have this barbecue? To thank our friends for helpin' build a barn. The dance is part of the thank-you as well, but the war thinned the crop of young men considerably. Women like Rose Bannion feel their loss heaviest when their neighbors lead out their husbands and dance. What sort of reward is it for good people to sit idly and watch others enjoy themselves?"

"I'm not very good company," Willie explained. "I've got a temper, and I say the wrong things. I never learned a gentle way to talk, and most of the women I've known could ride a horse and shoot a gun better'n they could bake or sew. As for dancing, I can't remember the last time I took a woman's hand and led her out to proper music. Was likely in Richmond back in '64. A few years've passed since then.''

"Well, I can't curb your temper, Willie Delamer, but I can certainly help you practice your steps. I suspect Elyssia could stand the practice as well. Between those Cobb boys, they always wear her down to a nub at barn dances."

"I guess I'm in your hands then, Elvira."

"I didn't offer you much choice, did I? Well, thank me later. There's another matter for us to work out."

"Yes?" Willie asked.

"You can't very well expect a civilized woman like Rose Bannion to pass the evening with a buckskin-clad bronc buster like yourself. You'll need a shave and a clippin' first of all. You tend the first, and I'll tackle the second. As for clothes, well . . .''

"I'd best pay a visit to town," Willie concluded. "I need some shirts and trousers for certain. Near everything I owned flew off in the storm. Mostly the shirts had worn elbows and the trousers were thin in the knees. I guess maybe I ought to have a look at some boots. And a new hat."

"I believe that would make a considerable improvement," Elvira agreed. "I'm not one for buryin' the past, mind, but it's best not to stare at it every moment."

"Stockings and undergarments'll be needed, too."

"And a string tie," she added. "You'll have no trouble finding everything in Albany. Thin as you are, I'd bet the Smith brothers can fit you from stock. I imagine it'll cost a pretty penny, though. Have you any money, Willie? I'm certain Ted hasn't paid you for your efforts here, and Travis Cobb certainly owes you something for the days you worked his ranch."

"You've all paid me more'n you can ever know," Willie replied. "And as for money, well, I had some luck at cards a while back."

"The bill could come to twenty or thirty dollars."

"Ma'am, in Colorado that's eating money. Never you mind about that. Trust me to have it in hand."

"Then you best hurry yourself along," Elvira concluded.

"I have a dinner to cook tonight, and we'll need time to practice the dance steps."

"Yes, ma'am," Willie said, grinning as he turned and headed toward the ready corral. In no time at all he had Stinger saddled, and shortly thereafter he was riding toward Albany.

Once in town, Willie hurried to the mercantile. The Smith brothers supplied the required clothing in short order, and Willie made his way over to the jailhouse.

" 'Mornin', Major," Grandpa Little said when Willie stepped to the clerk's counter. "Figured you'd be busy out at the Cobb place."

"Oh, they seem to have the building in hand," Willie declared. "Truth is, Ted Slocum's had me working horses this week. I suppose they don't trust me with a hammer."

"Want to thank you for takin' Tim in hand. Boy needs a man to measure himself against, and I've got a few too many gray hairs for the job."

"That right?" Willie asked. "That youngster doesn't say three words but that one of 'em's about you, Mr. Little. I'd say you're helping him to measure up just fine."

"Well, I do try," Little admitted. "What can I do for you today?"

"I thought maybe there might have been some dealings with Mr. Fairchild's land holdings."

"Now that's a funny thing," the clerk said, tapping his fingers. "I'd thought so, too, but so far there's been nothin' at all. Could be he hasn't gotten 'round to sellin'. Or else there's no buyer. Land's cheap these days, what with all that acreage out west openin' up."

"Maybe so," Willie muttered. "Makes for an uneasy night's sleep, though, knowing there's a rattlesnake about."

"I wouldn't worry a whole lot. Most all the county's goin' out to put up a barn at the Cobb place tomorrow. After that they'll be stuffin' themselves and dancin' to distraction at Slocum's."

"They won't stay there," Willie pointed out.

"No, but some'll be too drunk to head straight home, and others'll stay on for a week or two to help out."

109

"That's a comfort," Willie confessed.

He returned to the TS Ranch a bit before dinner. He barely got washed before Elvira was serving platters of pork chops and mounds of potatoes. Willie was unusually hungry, and he helped himself to a second plate of food. Afterward, while Lewis and Lamar were tending to the dishes, Elvira began Willie's dancing lesson.

He felt peculiar at first. Elvira had a grace to her movements, and Willie felt awkward by comparison.

"Guess it's hopeless," Willie observed after a half hour. "Just call me stumble foot."

"Nonsense," she said, lifting his chin. "I've seen you on horseback, Willie. Any man who can ride with such rhythm can dance any step he chooses. Let's try again with some music."

Elvira left for a moment. When she returned, she brought along a trio of cowboys. Two held fiddles, and a third carried a guitar. They soon filled the house with music, and Elvira took Willie's hand and began a waltz.

The music made all the difference. Willie's feet moved with new rhythm, and his timing soon meshed with Elvira's. Later on Elyssia took a turn. By nightfall the whole family was dancing—even Hood and Hill.

It was, however, a different story Saturday night when Willie and Rose Bannion paired up. The widow was as lovely as Lamar and Ted had said, and she had a manner that set Willie at ease.

"I'm afraid you must think me the desperate widow set out to rope a husband," she told him when they joined the other dancers. "Elvira, no doubt, has told you a thousand lies."

"I'd judge she didn't say half of it," Willie countered. "I know you lost your husband on the trail to Kansas, but you don't seem to've given up. Two girls and a boy I hear you're raising. That's a fair-sized job for anybody, and you run a farm to boot."

"Not well, I fear."

"Better than I would," Willie grumbled.

The beat of the music changed from moderate to fast then,

and the others turned to a livelier step. Willie had trouble from the start, and he soon trampled the widow Bannion proper. She merely laughed it off and urged him to try again. But Willie had no luck with the dance, and he soon surrendered.

"I'm no good at this," Willie told her. "Maybe you'd like to take another partner."

"I don't have to dance," she said, leading him past the new barn toward the river. "Actually, Major Delamer, I quite enjoy a walk. Particularly when the stars are out."

"They are," Willie observed. "All of them. There's nothing like a clear sky in autumn. Or anytime, for that matter. Makes a man small, I suppose, and that's good. Some have a bad habit of thinking themselves a hair taller than they are."

"And some think less of themselves than's due," she declared. "I think maybe you have that tendency."

"Me?" Willie asked, laughing. "No, I know just what I am."

"And what's that?"

"Oh, not a farmer. That's for sure. Nothing I ever planted grew to be eating size. I'm sort of a stray pup, you might say. Mostly a wanderer. Shoot, I've covered more country the past year than most people ever dream of seeing. I've hunted buffalo with Comanche Indians, herded cows to Kansas, hunted killers in Colorado, and been nigh killed by bluecoat cavalry in the Dakotas."

"But you weren't always a drifter. I know of your family."

"I've got no family," Willie told her. "Oh, I have relatives and such, but I don't know 'em. And they wouldn't know me to stare at my face. My own sister had me in her house a few months back and didn't recognize it was me."

"I don't believe that."

"I've changed some since I was fifteen," he explained. "Not a bit for the better, either."

"You fought in the war. It changed many men."

"Killed a fair portion, too. Cooled most of us toward killing, or else it hollowed us out. But all that's past."

"I notice you bought a new hat. When you came to town a few weeks back, my son Miles pointed you out to me.

'Look, Ma, there's a soldier,' he said. All I saw was the gray hat. And those sad eyes."

"Felt sorry, did you?"

"No, I merely recognized loneliness," she explained, gripping his hand with her own. "Maybe we can find a place to sit a while."

"No, it's turned late," Willie observed. "You have your little ones to mind, and my day starts early."

"Have I done something wrong?" she asked as he stepped away.

"No, you've been more'n kind, ma'am," Willie assured her. "It's me. I'm not fit for civilized company. Told Elvira as much, but bless her heart, she was so determined to try and reform me."

"I think you've done rather well," Mrs. Bannion argued. "If you'd care to try another waltz . . ."

"Wouldn't change anything," Willie told her. "I've been too long among wild things. And wild places. I understand 'em. I fit in there."

"Men can change."

"And they do all the time. But not often for the better. I didn't."

"But we'll see each other again. You haven't even met the children. Miles was so anxious to ask about your horse, and—"

"Wouldn't work," Willie said, shaking his head. "You need a steady man for the planting, and for the little ones, too. I'd be a rogue mustang, off hunting or scaring up trouble."

"That's truly too bad," she said, sighing. "I like you."

"You don't know me, ma'am. If you did, you'd find less to please yourself."

"I wish you'd let me discover that for myself."

"Trust me to know," Willie said as he walked her back to the dancing. "I wish you the best. Isn't often a woman opens her heart to a vagabond like me. Lord's sure to treat such a saint kindly."

She laughed at his joke, then kissed his cheek before leaving. He sadly watched her go, knowing when he took to his bed that he would feel lonelier than ever. But that would pass. He had the horses to tend, and work was always a good cure for an ailing heart.

CHAPTER 14

Others had a much better time at the dance. The Smith brothers had provided several jugs of a homemade peach wine, and more than one guest returned to Albany in the bed of a neighbor's wagon.

"Stuff's potent," Travis Cobb observed.

"Sure it is," Ted Slocum agreed. "A notch short o' blastin' powder."

Among the sufferers was young Gus Slocum. The nineteen-year-old was green as a turnip, and it took his father and all four brothers to cart him to the house.

"Funny how a little o' that juice can make you feel good and a hair more'll burn your insides out," Jess said, laughing as Davy tried futilely to mount his horse.

"Best help him into the wagon with the little ones," Travis advised. "Foggy-eyed like he is, he's sure to run smack into a tree."

As for Willie, he figured to pass another night at the Slocum ranch, but Travis had other thoughts.

"Got you a nice place fixed up in the new barn," Travis declared. "Irene's stitched you up a quilt to brace you against a mornin' chill, and Mike stuffed a mattress with chicken feathers so it'd be nice and soft."

"It is, too," Little Tim declared. "I tried it out last night."

"I'm not yet finished with these horses o' Ted's," Willie argued.

"Nonsense," Elvira Slocum said, helping a weary Josh Cobb into the wagon alongside Davy. "Horse'll wait. It's not but a short ride back here anyway, and that Stinger's got plenty of run in him."

"I'll get my gear," Willie said, surrendering.

"It's your own fault," Bobby said, grinning dizzily. "Had to get yourself fancied up. All the women'll be after you now. New hat did it!"

The others had a good laugh. Willie merely sighed.

It took a few minutes to saddle Stinger and bid farewell to the Slocum youngsters. He had parting words for some of the townfolk as well. Finally he climbed atop an agitated Stinger and joined the Cobbs for the short ride homeward.

"You lead the way, Trav," Jesse suggested. "Ole Bobby and I'll bring up the rear. I got a feelin' Bob might need to make a stop or two 'long the way."

"He's drunk," Mike cackled. "Near as bad as Davy."

"Am not," Bobby replied. "Was only celebratin' my arm bein' well."

"More likely toastin' Elyssia," Jesse argued. "Anyhow, lead off, Trav."

"And me?" Willie asked.

"Best come along with us," Jesse said with what might pass as a smile. "We probably need protectin'."

"Sure, you do," Willie agreed. "From another jug of that peach wine."

As the high-spirited procession rolled along, Bobby took up a tune. Irene devoted several minutes to a discourse on the evils of strong spirits while Mike and Tim Little mimicked Bobby's hoarse attempts at song making. They were almost home when the moon broke over the distant hills, showering the trail with pale light.

"Be a bright night," Travis declared as he pointed to the moon. "Makes for some fine tale-spinnin'."

"Bet Uncle Wil knows one or two he'd share," Mike remarked.

"Sure, he does," Tim added. "You'll tell us one 'fore we

have to take to our beds, won't you? I got to go back to town in the mornin', and Grandpa's sure to have me slavin' at chores for the next week to make up for all the time I been out here."

"Seems late already," Willie noted.

"Please, Uncle Wil?" Tim pleaded.

"Am I everybody's uncle now?" Willie asked.

"Just about," Travis admitted. "These small fry've gone and adopted you, Willie."

"A short one wouldn't hurt," Irene said. "They've truly been working hard to get your bed ready. And it's not so late as it might be."

"One story," Willie announced. "But then it's to bed, eh?"

Josh managed to lift his head long enough to flash a grin. Mike and Tim cheered.

The day might and should have ended on such a high note, but it wasn't to be. The singular crack of a rifle shot fractured the calm, and the world descended into a nightmare.

"Bushwhackers!" Jesse shouted as he raced past Willie to the wagon.

"Get 'em home!" Willie yelled as he pulled his Winchester from its saddle scabbard and leaped to cover. A volley tore through the nearby trees, showering the trail with wood splinters and rock fragments. Travis whipped his team into a gallop, and Willie watched with grim satisfaction as the wagon vanished in a ridge of smoke.

"Major, where you got to?" Bobby then called.

Willie went cold inside. Bobby stood alone in the trail, framed by the moon's silvery glow.

"Get down!" Willie shouted as he rushed toward the young man. The ambushers found Bobby first. A dozen bullets whined through the air. More than one found its mark, and Bobby's horse screamed into the night.

Willie reached the writhing animal and managed to drag its rider off to the cover of a nearby juniper.

"They come back," Bobby muttered.

"So it'd seem," Willie agreed, recalling how Grandpa Little had thought trouble so unlikely. Why'd I listen? Willie asked himself. Why didn't we finish that Englishman when we had the chance?

"Did Trav get away?" Bobby asked as shots peppered the tree overhead.

"I think so," Willie answered. "Jesse was covering him, and I don't hear any shooting in that direction."

"Fine thing," Bobby grumbled. "Get my arm to where I can use it, and this happens."

"You hit?" Willie asked.

"Left leg," the younger man explained. "Just below the knee. I'm not hurt so bad I can't shoot, though."

Willie offered Bobby a pistol, then had a look at the battered leg. Already blood was soaking through Bobby's trousers. Willie tore the fabric and saw a pair of nasty wounds. He ripped his shirt into strips and bound them both. Then he took his rifle and set about the business of exacting payment.

"They's down past the trail there!" a bushwhacker announced.

"Martley, finish them!" an all-too-familiar voice commanded.

Willie heard footsteps rustling through the high grass, and he swung his rifle in that direction. Two shadows moved across the moonlit hillside, and Willie fired four shots. One man spun backward. The second screamed in pain.

"He's holed up there good!" Leon Martley announced. "It'd take a stick o' dynamite to pry him loose!"

"Well, we don't have any, do we?" Fairchild grumbled. "You do have some expensive help. Get it done, Martley!"

Willie was ready when a second pair started in from the right, and Bobby fired as well. The shots sent the cautious gunmen retreating.

"Get him!" Fairchild ordered.

"He's got the edge!" Martley argued. "Better we head up to the house and finish the ones there."

"No!" Bobby said, sitting up and firing rapidly toward the voices.

"Get down!" Willie shouted, fighting to drag Bobby to cover. The gun flashes were like signposts, and rifles barked. Bullets spattered the tree. One sliced through the brim of

Willie's new hat, and a second nicked his right boot. Bobby uttered a mute cry and fell in a heap at Willie's elbow.

"Young fool," Willie said, cradling his fallen friend's head. "Did a fine job of it this time, didn't you."

"Expect so," Bobby said, coughing.

Fairchild's men made a fresh charge, but Willie emptied the Winchester's magazine at them, and they took to their heels.

"Charge!" Fairchild screamed. "We've got him now."

But the hirelings had seen enough. Or perhaps they heard the storm of hooves heading along the river. Even as Willie fought to reload his rifle, the skulking raiders were heading for safer surroundings.

"How bad is it?" Willie asked when he was confident the attack had failed.

"Bad enough," Bobby answered. The young man opened his shirt, and Willie ran his hand along the exposed flesh. His fingers came away wet and sticky. Willie edged Bobby's bleeding frame over so the moonlight fell across the tortured youngster's face. Already the boyish eyes were glassy.

Willie paled as he saw the rest. One bullet had pierced Bobby's side below the rib cage and torn into the vitals. Willie ripped what remained of his shirt into new strips and tried to plug the hole, but already Bobby was coughing blood. Lung shot, Willie thought.

"Don't bother 'bout me," Bobby said, wincing as Willie tried to stem the blood flow. "I know. My feet've gone numb already. Have a look after Trav."

"He's all right," Willie said reassuringly. "I heard horses coming. Help's arrived, and the snakes have turned tail."

"Why not?" Bobby said, coughing violently. "They done the job."

"Be another day!" Martley suddenly screamed across the darkness.

"No, not for me," Bobby mumbled as he stared faintly toward Willie.

There really wasn't much to be done. Willie tightened the bindings, hoping to corral the bleeding, but Bobby was clearly coughing out his life. By the time Travis and Jesse arrived, it was nearly over.

"Bobby?" Jesse cried, sitting at his brother's side. "Lord, wasn't gettin' shot once enough for you?"

"Didn't take the last time," Bobby muttered. "This time, well, Cobbs never been known for doin' things halfway. Know any prayers, Jess? I can't seem to remember any."

"One or two," Jesse said, cradling his brother's head and whispering the words. The two prayed solemnly while Willie stared helplessly at Travis. The encroaching fingers of death drew near.

"It's a funny thing," Bobby suddenly said, intertwining the fingers of his hands with those of his brothers. "I always figured it would hurt worse'n this. Shoot, ain't even as bad as when they hit my arm."

"Hush," Jesse pleaded with tearful eyes.

"Save your strength," Travis urged.

"For what?" Bobby asked. "I got things to say. Jess, you'll remember? Trav?"

"I'll remember," Jesse promised.

"Go ahead on," Travis added.

"I want Mike should have my silver belt buckle. My horse, too, if you can find it. I got a metal box hid 'neath my bunk. There's some things o' Pa's in it and a locket Ma gave me. Give 'em to Irene for to keep for Josh and Art. Maybe she'll give you a girl sometime, Trav. Little gal'd fancy that locket."

"You'll be here to give it to her on her weddin' day," Travis argued.

"I'll be hereabouts, but under sand and rock. Major got some o' the ones who shot me, though. They're in for a fiery time of it if Ma was right. If you find them fellows on yon hill, you won't put us in the ground together, will you? I heard of it bein' done."

"He's buzzard bait by noon tomorrow," Jesse growled.

"And me? I'd like to rest up on that hill above where we race the river, Trav. Like to think o' Cobb boys swimmin' there and thinkin' 'bout me some."

"Bobby . . ."

"There's somethin' else," Bobby said, struggling with great effort to gaze toward Willie. "Major, I saw . . ."

"Bobby?" Jesse cried as the words suddenly stopped. Bobby stared a moment toward the sky, then muttered a cry of surprise. Blood trickled out of the corner of his mouth, and his chest sank.

"No!" Jesse shouted, shaking Bobby's still body as if that might restore life. "No!"

"He's not there," Travis said, grasping Jesse by both shoulders.

"No!" Jesse repeated. "No!"

Willie bent down and gently closed Bobby's eyelids. Willie'd seen death a hundred times or more, but it never failed to shake him. He didn't see a bloody twenty-one-year-old, after all. Bobby Cobb was the same child who'd ridden behind him on a rogue mustang, who had sat patiently beside Willie and learned to work hides. Here lay the boy who had tearfully bid Travis off to join the army.

Willie touched the boy's forehead and found it cold.

"Was it Fairchild?" Travis asked bitterly. "Did you see or hear anything?"

"Plenty," Willie said coldly.

"We could take proof to Sheriff Pennypacker," Travis suggested.

"What'd he do?" Jesse asked, taking the stiffening body of his younger brother in his trembling arms and starting for the house.

"He's right," Willie declared, gazing somberly into Travis's burning eyes. "I was wrong to leave Fairchild a way out. Trav, it's doing! Lord, I'd do it over if there was the chance. It's just that I'm so tired of all this killing!"

"I know, Willie," Travis said, gripping his old friend's wrists. "We'll settle accounts with Fairchild later. There's some boys up to the house needin' a story."

"I can't," Willie cried.

"They need to know things'll work out," Travis argued. "They need some comfort . . . and distraction. They need to feel safe."

"Are they?" Willie asked. "Is anybody?"

"They got us to make it so," Travis answered. "We will, too. I promise you that."

Willie nodded. And even as he sat in the barn, inhaling the odor of fresh-hewn juniper planks as he told the little ones a tale of chasing ponies on the Sweetwater River, he vowed to find Romney Fairchild and Leon Martley and see they bled as Bobby Cobb had. It was a promise that screamed through his mind. It would be kept.

CHAPTER 15

Willie Delamer couldn't recall a longer night. He never found more than a few minutes' rest. He kept seeing Bobby's pale face, saw Trav's grief-stricken eyes, and blamed himself for the death that had struck so close.

"It's my doing," Willie said when he stood beside Travis that next morning washing up for breakfast. "Me and my ideas! I thought if only we could shame Fairchild, hold him up for others to see, that'd be the end of it."

"I went along easy enough," Travis pointed out. "As for Bobby, he favored it with all his heart. He was always one for a well-done prank, and seein' that Englishman prancin' into the Flat decked out in his silk drawers was somethin' to remember."

"Wasn't worth the cost," Willie declared.

"You didn't call this tune, Willie," Travis argued. "This is my fight, mine and Ted's."

"You forget it was me shot the son, put an end to his game at Myra's. He may want your land, or the high water crossing anyway, but it's me he wants dead."

"Killin' you's not the easiest job to get done, though. Better men've tried."

"And worse," Willie muttered. "You know Fairchild'll be back to make you an offer. What'll you do?"

"Make a stand," Travis answered. "I left one place. This

122

land here's been paid for with sweat, and now with blood. Art and Josh were born here. It's worth a fight.''

Willie nodded his agreement.

He couldn't force a bite of breakfast down himself, and he left the table early. Jesse and Davy likewise failed to eat. Even the little ones seemed shaken. though perhaps for them it was their father's clouded brow that brought alarm. As for Jesse and Davy, they kept busy digging a grave beside their father's simple picket cross.

''Tim rode into Albany to fetch Preacher Shapcott,'' Mike explained a bit later. ''We'll do the buryin' soon's he gets here. Can't keep a body fresh long this time o' year.''

''You'd know about that, would you?'' Willie asked.

''I seen plenty o' men kilt,'' Mike explained. ''By cows and storms and Comanches. More'n a few by bullets. Ma and me lived at Fort Griffin Town 'fore she married Pa.''

''Hard thing, growing up around death,'' Willie said bitterly.

''Pa says it's knowin' death's at hand gives life such a high value. Said you told him that back in Virginia.''

''Yeah?'' Willie asked. I've learned a lot since then, he thought.

Tim Little returned to the ranch a bit shy of midday. Behind him Grandpa Little drove an open-bed wagon filled with food and drink. Baptist preacher Ramper Shapcott and his wife followed in a second wagon, leading a procession of buggies and freight wagons filled with women and children. Fathers and husbands rode along the flanks.

''Lord, the whole county's come,'' Jesse gasped.

''Good thing they brought food with 'em,'' Davy said, attempting a grin. ''Never saw so many folks in one place before.''

''Takes a buryin' to bring people together,'' Irene observed. ''Well, I don't suppose this'll be the last one.''

No, Willie told himself. Likely not.

The burying began moments later after Ted Slocum and his family joined the mourners. The Slocums, Gus and Elyssia in particular, were shaken. They stepped to Irene's side

123

and offered words of consolation. Or tried, anyway. Mostly they cried.

Little was spoken of the midnight terror, of devil-eyed Leon Martley or Romney Fairchild. There was only the sad specter of Bobby Cobb's slender body carried along to the grave by his mournful brothers and nephew Mike. Irene lovingly wrapped the lifeless form in the folds of a twenty-year-old quilt. Then Travis and Jesse gently lowered it into the earth.

"We gather today to usher Robert Cobb to his eternal reward," Ramper Shapcott spoke. Willie thought "Rambler" would have been a better name for the man, as he seemed to stretch the short memorial into a small eternity. The children scratched their stiff collars or pawed the ground with their feet. A few of the elderly dozed off.

"Thanks for your kind words, Reverend Shapcott," Travis finally announced. "And thank you all for comin'. Bobby favored singin', and I'd ask you to join us in a song or two to comfort those left behind."

The family then led the singing of calls for glory and gathering at rivers. Willie had no heart for it. He sat on a juniper stump and stared at the river relentlessly bubbling along. Neither the preacher's readings nor the singing swept any of the bitterness from Willie's heart. No, he was recalling his vow. And figuring out how best Fairchild might be brought to bay.

"They call you the major, I'll bet," a large, white-haired man dressed in a black cutaway coat called as he stepped to Willie's side. "I'm Nate Pennypacker."

"That's a name I've heard before," Willie said, taking the man's hand. "The sheriff?"

"Yes, sir," Pennypacker said, pulling his coat back to reveal a pewter star affixed to a vest beneath. "I've been meanin' to have some words with you over a bit of shootin' out to the Flat. Boy named Fairchild got kilt there."

"And another man, as I recall," Willie added. "Near took a bullet myself."

"I understand it was on account o' cards."

"Young Fairchild and his father were stacking the odds,

Sheriff. Oh, I know a man takes his chances walking into another fellow's town, but I can't abide doctoring cards. I turned the tables on 'em, so to speak, and they didn't take it with grace.''

"As I heard it, you pulled a gun," Pennypacker declared.

"I didn't make the first move," Willie insisted. "And I never fired till they opened up. Must be plenty who saw it and would say so.''

"Couldn't you slide back from such trouble?" the sheriff asked.

"I slid back a few weeks ago, Sheriff," Willie said, frowning. "Now Bobby Cobb lies dead. I don't know it's altogether smart to leave a gun pointed at your back when you mount a horse. Can make for a short life."

"For somebody," Pennypacker observed. "I'd caution you to stay clear o' trouble in my county from here on out."

"Sheriff, don't you figure you might be preaching to the wrong fellow? I was with Bobby when he was shot. I saw and heard that English fellow Fairchild order it done. I saw Leon Martley there, too."

"I spoke with the both of 'em. Said they was holed up past Fort Griffin. Got witnesses to swear it so."

"Lie, you mean," Willie muttered. "Well, next time they come this way, I'll be settling accounts. You share that with 'em, would you?"

The sheriff started to argue, but Willie abandoned his stump and strolled out to the river. He remained alone for half an hour. Then Jesse and Elyssia brought over a plate of food.

"He was my brother," Jesse declared.

"I loved him," Elyssia added. "He's gone now, though. You have to let him be."

"I have," Willie said, nodding solemnly at the two young people. "It's not mourning's brought me to the river. It's knowing what's bound to happen next."

"And what's that?" Elyssia asked.

"Death. More dying. Guns blasting riders from the range. Bullets tearing through little kids. A blood plague that'll sweep through this valley and stain it forever."

"You've fought such wars before," Jesse said. "Les told me so. Up in the Cimarron country and in the Colorado goldfields. I've heard drifters in the Flat talk about Billy Starr."

"He's dead," Willie declared. "I turned away from him."

"Bring him back," Elyssia said with hard, cruel eyes. "He's needed."

Willie felt his insides grow cold to see such anger. Travis was no better, either. He raged at the sheriff for accepting Fairchild's tale and demanded justice.

"Justice is where you find it," Grandpa Little asserted. "Or buy it."

Pennypacker took real offense at the slur, but he found no one to rush to his defense. He muttered a warning, mounted his horse, and headed back to Albany. A chorus of jeers followed him.

"May come to regret that," Ted Slocum said. "Wouldn't hurt to have the law at our side."

"Pennypacker?" Jesse cried. "He's no law. People at the Flat wanted a sheriff for Shackleford County that wouldn't bother their business. You'll note he stays in Albany, where the biggest problem he's apt to find's a stubbed toe. Even if he had proof, he wouldn't ride out to see Fairchild, much less arrest anybody."

"He's at least got some sense," Willie declared. "That'd just get him dead."

The talk moved to other topics for a bit. Farmers devoted to harvesting drought-stunted corn had too much work awaiting them to remain idle for long. The neighbors began drifting off. In an hour's time most of the visitors were gone. That's when Romney Fairchild appeared.

Others might have noticed the horses first. Willie heard the hated squeal of buggy wheels. He grabbed his Winchester and raced up the hill to the house. Fairchild and Martley were waiting there.

"You're not welcome here!" Jesse screamed from the porch. "Murderer! What manner o' gumption brings you here today of all days!"

"Heard you come by some misfortune," Martley answered. "Mr. Fairchild just wanted to pass on his sympathies."

"We'd as soon Mr. Fairchild just pass on," Elyssia Slocum retorted. "If I had a gun in my hand, you'd be dyin', mister!"

"I've got one," Willie added, raising the barrel of the Winchester. "Fairchild, I'd get out of here if I was you. I'd hate to make this day any bloodier than it is already, but—"

"Put down the gun, friend," Martley advised.

"I'm no manner of friend to you!" Willie barked.

"I'd do as Leon suggests," Fairchild said, grinning as he motioned toward the distant stands of junipers. Riders suddenly emerged from cover until a dozen or so formed a loose circle around the house. At the river ragged drifters held rifles on visiting children. Art and Josh Cobb clung to Mike's sides.

"You stupid enough to start a war with fifty people watching?" Willie asked.

"Oh, I'm not starting a thing," Fairchild explained." I'm ending our disagreements here and now. Look around you, sirs. Do you see how easily an accident might kill a child? Or two. Or even a whole brood. I just wished to make a point. These river crossings can prove quite dangerous. They'll bring all manner of unwelcome attention. Why not leave them in the hands of a man who knows how to hire work done?"

"Killin', you mean," Jesse accused.

"Now that's hardly friendly," Fairchild said, and a rifle barked. A rifle ball exploded against the wall of the house, showering Jesse with splinters.

"You've made your precious point," Slocum said, scowling. "What is it exactly you want?"

"The crossings, together with an adjoining strip that will merge with my holdings elsewhere. Didn't I make that plain?" Fairchild asked.

"And if I don't agree?" Travis asked.

"We'll be back," Martley threatened.

Willie gazed at the line of grim-faced figures on horseback. There wasn't a hint of pity to be found in those somber

127

eyes. They were too young by half to find themselves in a range war, but their tattered clothes and undernourished bodies spoke of quiet desperation. A desperate man was the worst kind of enemy. He fought to the end because he didn't care what happened.

Willie froze when he reached the end of the line. There, dressed in patchwork britches and a ragged yellow shirt, was a sandy-haired urchin of fourteen or so. Gil? Willie silently asked, recalling the boy from his earlier visit to the Flat. The boy's eyes blinked recognition, but they offered no sign of truce.

"Well, Cobb?" Martley shouted. "Slocum? Care to come to terms or fight?"

"There'll be no fight here, not today!" Preacher Shapcott shouted as he trotted over to intercede. "Not here! Not now! Do you men hear me?"

"We hear you," Travis said, glaring at Fairchild.

"Shut your yappin', old man," Martley warned.

"Listen to me," Shapcott went on to say. "Settle your differences if you must, but not here, so close to God's hallowed ground. 'Vengeance is Mine!' He hath taught us. So it is He will strike down the evil and raise up the good."

"You callin' me evil, Preacher?" Martley said, pulling his pistol in a flash and shooting Shapcott's broad-brimmed hat off his head. "How's that for good work, eh?"

The riders hooted, and Shapcott, clearly shaken by his brush with immortality, took refuge behind his wagon. Martley prepared to fire again, but Willie lifted his rifle.

"Are you that big of a fool, Fairchild?" Willie asked. "Hasn't there been enough death here?"

"A dozen men would drop you," Martley warned Willie.

"You and your boss'd be dead, though," Willie argued. "I'd see to that. All in all it might not be such a bad bargain, my hide for yours."

Fairchild read Willie's face and motioned for Martley to holster the pistol.

"You've a decision to make," the Englishman announced, turning to Travis and Ted Slocum. "I'll give you two days' time to consider. When I return, it will be to complete our bargain . . . or to commence a different nature of negotiation.''

"Why wait?" Travis shouted. "I won't be alterin' my opinions."

"You might," Martley said. "The boss can be mighty persuasive."

Can he? Willie wondered. Well, they didn't altogether know it, but so could Willie.

CHAPTER 16

"What's to be done now?" Travis asked an hour later when the last of the neighbors had left.

"Way I see it," Jesse said, "we can either sell out or fight. No choice, to be truthful. Bobby's already in the ground. It's war, pure and simple."

"Nothin's ever simple, nor pure, either," Travis argued. "What do you think, Willie?"

"I think I'm the wrong man to ask," Willie responded. "But since you've done it, I'll speak my mind. This Fairchild's been off scraping together every pair of hands he can find. Shoot, there were boys of fourteen with him today. He can say he's given us two days to ponder things, but all he's really done is wangled some time for him to get himself organized. Can't give 'em that time, Trav. We got to carry the fight to him. Strike hard and fast like in the war. Keep him off balance."

"How?" Jesse asked. "He's got us outnumbered. We don't even know where he is!"

"We will," Willie answered. "By dusk."

"Where are you headin'?" Travis asked as Willie walked toward the corral.

"I've spent a lot of years riding this country," Willie explained. "I'd guess there're three men ever lived who could track a man in this rock-hard ground. The other two are dead now. I'll find Fairchild's camp. And then we'll plan how to put an end to this nightmare!"

Travis voiced concerns aplenty.

"Why not bide our time a bit?" he asked. "The boys need a rest."

"Two reasons you can't delay," Willie explained. "First, you won't really be able to drop your guard, not knowing Fairchild for the liar he is. Second, they won't be idle. Those untried boys'll stiffen their resolve once they get used to the notion of taking us on. Show 'em it's apt to cost lives, and some'll leave before you can shake a stick at 'em."

"Be careful," Travis urged as Willie saddled Stinger. "They won't leave you an easy trail to follow."

"No, but then I never needed one. It's hard to hide a dozen men."

"Or even one," Travis noted. "Watch out for bushwhackers."

"Always do," Willie assured his old friend. "You keep a guard posted here, too. And especially around the little ones. We've dug enough graves."

And so Willie set out after Fairchild's riders. In the beginning he found a good assortment of tracks. The soft ground watered by the river and its myriad feeder streams made tracing the raiders easy. Later, as the horsemen headed across the hard limestone ridges and through sandy ravines, they nearly vanished. An untrained eye would never have noticed the broken twig, the scrap of cotton snared by a cactus thorn, or the leavings from an emptied smoker's pipe. Those clues kept Willie closing the distance between himself and the quarry.

The first hint of darkness was falling across the land when Willie wound his way up a slope and beheld a huddle of outbuildings not far from the river. The place appeared familiar. Willie scratched his head and searched his memory. Then something stirred in the high grass behind him.

Willie instantly pulled a pistol and spun. The long barrel of the Colt trained squarely on the forehead of young Gil, the horse tender he'd brought out of the Flat weeks before.

"Didn't mean to startle you, General," Gil said, turning

131

out his empty pockets. "You can have a closer look if you want. I got no gun."

"What're you doing here?" Willie asked.

"Waitin' for you, o' course," the boy said, stepping closer. "See you traded in the pinto. This one's got a fast look to him. Bet he'll run all day."

"Gil!"

"I figured you to come along," the boy explained. "Read it in your eyes."

"Why sign on with Fairchild? Don't you know he's the worst sort? You've turned your hands to a poor trade, I'm thinking."

"I didn't plan it. You brought me out here yourself, or did you forget? Fairchild come out and bought the place a while back. Took the stock, the buildin's, every last stitch o' the place. I suppose you'd say I got throwed in on the deal. No place to go, and no people to worry after me."

"And now?" Willie asked. "Do they know you're up here?"

"No, and it won't exactly warm 'em to my hide. They ain't particular fond o' me anyhow."

Gil unbuttoned his shirt and showed off welts left by a leather strap on his ribs and back.

"I'll not have you go back there," Willie announced. "I've got a friend, Ted Slocum, who could probably use another stable boy."

"Would you recommend me to him?"

"I would. Gil, do you have some things to fetch from yon camp?"

"Nothin' you'd want to keep."

"Wait for me here," Willie said, nodding his understanding. "I want to have a look around."

"No, not on horseback," the boy warned. "You want me to show you a way in? Hop off and I'll lead the way."

Willie did as instructed. He was surprised to discover Gil so adept at winding his way down ravines and through brush toward the ranch buildings.

"They call this the Crown Ranch," the boy whispered as he walked. "Mr. Fairchild, he says his people were kings or

132

dukes or some such nonsense. We been brandin' critters with a crown mark. Me, I'll always think of it bein' the Shanklin place.''

"What became of the Shanklins?" Willie asked.

"Left in a sudden hurry," Gil answered nervously. "Littlest gal broke her leg, and Johnny, their boy, nigh drowned in a pond. Bad luck, all that comin' along so quick.''

"I don't figure either hurt was altogether accidental.''

"You figure right. Was about the same sort o' accident'd happen if you walked ten more feet down this trail. Guard'd shoot you dead.''

"Guard?" Willie asked. "What guard?"

"The one hidin' in the rocks there on the right. See? Got the barrel o' his Winchester leakin' out o' the trees.''

"So, that's the real reason you were waiting," Willie said, shaking his head sourly. "To save my hide.''

"I recall how you stood up for me at the Flat. Wasn't anything else I could do but return the favor. I pay my debts, you know.''

"I do now," Willie said, mustering a smile. "Suppose we take a closer peek at the ranch.''

"This way," Gil whispered, creeping to his left before descending a rise and threading his way through thick brush until getting to within a stone's throw of a long picket structure.

"This would be the bunkhouse," Willie noted as he fixed the position in his mind.

"That yonder's the big house," Gil added. "Barn's there past the corrals.''

"How many men are here at night?"

"Whole outfit," Gil whispered, looking first to his left and then to his right. "Close to twenty of us now. Mostly just poor cowboys, you know. Wouldn't harm nobody if there was honest work to be had. Couple of 'em's bounty killers, though. You'd want to watch them. Then there's Martley. Was him whipped me. He got shot and turned himself mean. I remember him for a fair man at the Flat. Used to give me a dollar to mind his horse. Now, well, he's bent on killin'.''

"What do you know of Fairchild?"

"Nothin'," the boy said, his face paling. "I kept plenty clear o' him. Yes, sir, plenty clear!"

"Sure," Willie said, taking a final glance at the ranch buildings. "Best we be off now."

"This way," Gil suggested, slithering through the brush. Willie followed, and ten minutes later they reached Stinger unharmed. Willie mounted, then offered Gil a hand up. The sun had now passed from view, and darkness was settling quickly. It didn't much matter, of course. Willie was used to the dark, and Stinger knew the way home.

Back at the Cobb place, Jesse stood guard on the slope overlooking the river. As soon as Stinger splashed into the shallows to take a drink, Jesse hollered a challenge.

"It's all right!" Willie shouted in reply. "It's Wil."

"Good Lord, we've been worried after you," Jesse declared as he trotted down the hillside. "Trav went off lookin' for you, but he give up a while back. Said you and the night were old friends and got along better'n most married folk."

"Sounds like him," Willie said, managing a laugh. "I'm going over to the TS now, but I'll be back with some company in half an hour or so. We got ourselves some riding to do. Have everybody ready."

"Thought maybe it'd be tonight," Jesse noted sourly. "Heard you tell Trav how you wouldn't waste time."

"Odds are long already," Willie explained. "They'll get worse here on out."

Jesse nodded, and Willie turned Stinger westward. The horse splashed its way to the bank and hurried along to the Slocum place.

Ted Slocum had guards posted as well, and twice Willie had to answer challenges. Finally, when he appeared at the house, Gus Slocum set aside a shotgun and went to fetch his father. Gil, meanwhile, leaped down from Stinger's back.

"What's that you brought along with you?" Lamar asked when he and Lewis trotted out to the porch. "Field rat?"

"This here's Gil . . . shoot, I don't even know your whole name, boy!"

"It's Gilbert Cooksey," the youngster answered.

"Signin' him on as a gun hand, Uncle Wil?" Lewis asked. "Might be a hair small."

"He's done us a fair favor," Willie admonished his young friends. "Been down with Fairchild's company a bit. Not altogether comfortable there. Show 'em the lash marks, Gil. We met a bit back in the Flat, and I thought Gil had fallen on better times at the Shanklin place. Now it seems Fairchild's taken over there."

"That right?" Slocum asked, gazing at the boy from the doorway.

"Right, Mr. Slocum. Has twenty hands out that way, and some know their business. You remember me, don't you? I tended your horse a couple o' months back when you brought in that load o' cowhides for the Dermott brothers."

"Sure," Slocum said, nodding in recollection.

"Gil could use a job," Willie announced. "Claims to know horses, and he's got hawk's eyes for spotting trouble."

"He's awful little," Gus pointed out.

"He'll grow," Willie countered. "I figure he's done us a service worth reward, too. Says he pays his debts, this youngster. I got the same habit."

"Me too," Slocum added. "Lewis, find him a bunk. We got ourselves another hand."

"Thank you, Mr. Slocum," the boy answered. "And you, General."

"Gone and got promoted?" Slocum asked.

"Gil, try Willie instead," Willie suggested.

While Lewis conducted Gil to the bunkhouse, Willie told Slocum of the planned raid on Fairchild.

"Take most o' my crew to tackle twenty men," Slocum said, shaking his head. "I'd want to leave five or six to look after the ranch, and a couple more ought to watch Trav's place. I could muster ten hands, together with Gus and myself. Lamar and Lewis are—"

"Too young for what I've got in my head," Willie declared. "Ted, we've done plenty of raiding in our lifetimes. Won't be numbers that's needed. Surprise'll do the job, and young Gil there's given me the edge we need. I've scouted the camp. Looks like three guards and three buildings. I'd judge eight men'd do it just fine.''

''Oh?''

''Trav, Jess, Davy, you and Gus there, me and a pair of your steadiest hands.''

''Bart Wallace's been in a scrape or two,'' Gus said. ''And M. T. Hennigan. Good shot with a rifle.''

''Fetch 'em,'' Slocum ordered, and Gus trotted off to do just that. ''Long odds, wouldn't you think, Major?''

''Not tackling a Yank regiment,'' Willie observed. ''Mostly scared cowboys. I'd guess we'll be enough.''

''I trust you to know.''

Gus returned with Wallace, Hennigan, and four saddled horses. Slocum paused only long enough to bid Elvira and the younger boys farewell before mounting his horse and following Willie to the Cobb place. Two other hands trailed the group. Willie knew these two would guard Trav's family.

As for Travis himself, he, Jesse, and Davy stood beside their saddled horses, eager to avenge a fallen brother. Willie said nothing, just pointed to the trail ahead. The Cobb brothers fell into line, and the small company rode onward.

About a mile shy of the Shanklin ranch, Willie pulled up and held a brief council of war. He drew a sketch of sorts in the sandy trail and assigned each man a task. It wasn't easy seeing in the faint moonlight, but the others knew the Shanklin layout well enough, and each head in turn nodded its understanding of the task at hand.

Now came the time to carry out the raid. Willie and Travis led the way on foot as they'd done a dozen times before in Virginia. They easily identified the guards. The first was clubbed across the head and then bound. The other two were led into the brush by a few intentional sounds. Travis drove a knife into the lead man's back, and Willie knocked the other senseless with his pistol barrel.

Willie next motioned silently to Ted Slocum, and the rancher led Gus and Davy toward the horse corrals. In no time they slid rails aside and urged the horses out into the open.

"Hey, the horses!" a cowboy suddenly yelled from the bunkhouse steps.

The raiders screamed and slapped the horses into a gallop, and the animals fled for their lives. Jesse and the TS hands opened fire on the bunkhouse, driving Fairchild's hands to cover within the picket walls.

"Now the fun begins," Willie said as he led Travis toward the ranch house. Already yellow curls of flame leaped from where Ted's trio had lit the barn. Shortly the house, too, was glowing.

"Martley!" Fairchild screamed from the front window of the blazing house. "Martley, get some men over here!"

"We're trapped!" Martley answered from the bunkhouse.

"I'll pay a hundred dollars for every one of these arsonists that's killed!" Fairchild cried.

Willie grinned at the desperation seeping into Fairchild's voice. The attack was going well. Ted piled dry brush against the bunkhouse then and set it, too, afire. With the inferno erupting around them and Fairchild upping his offer by the minute, the trapped cowboys chose to try an escape. Someone threw a chair through the back window, and a dozen men scampered out that way. Hennigan dropped one with a rifle, and Wallace felled two more with a shotgun blast. Pistol and rifle fire took a further toll. One party of survivors managed to extricate Fairchild from the ruin of the house, but mostly the scared hands headed for open ground and kept going.

"So much for Fairchild," Travis said, laughing as he observed the cowering fugitives in a nearby ravine.

"No, we counted him finished once before," Willie argued. "He won't give up this easily."

It wasn't a minute before Fairchild proved how true that was.

"You may think you have won, but I continue to hold the high cards, gentlemen!" the Englishman yelled. "All you've done this night is burn a bit of lumber and disturb my sleep."

"That all?" Willie shouted. "Listen here, Fairchild. I warned you before. There's room here for everybody. Leave my friends be! Elsewise you won't find much sleep, because every time you close your eyes, I'll be visiting your dreams. Wait and see what a nightmare I'll become.''

"He's yonder in them trees!" a cowboy shouted, and Leon Martley limped over and took refuge behind a large stone well. He raised a rifle to his shoulder and opened a continuous, steady fire on the rise where Willie and Travis had crawled.

"You all right, Major?" Ted Slocum asked as he returned Martley's fire.

"Just fine," Willie said, firing his own shot toward where Fairchild huddled. The Englishman shrieked, and Willie grinned bitterly. Martley added a fresh taunt or two. Then a bucket of coal oil came flying out of nowhere toward the house. A yellow flash leaped up the front of the building, showering light on the crouching Martley. The gunman turned to flee and was caught by a terrific shotgun blast that obliterated him.

"He wasn't so much, was he?" Jesse Cobb called from the shadows. "You're next, Fairchild! Payment for my brother!"

For the first time terror replaced the fear in Romney Fairchild's voice. The would-be king of Clear Fork bolted. His men followed. Willie fired in the direction of their footsteps, but the night swallowed the fugitives, and there was nothing more that could be done.

"Missed the scoundrel!" Travis grumbled. "But at least we dropped Martley. And there won't be many of those cowboys stick."

"That's a help?" Willie asked. "Before we knew which faces to look out for. Now, well, it could turn out to be anyone. Anywhere. Anytime."

"Best keep our guard up," Slocum agreed.

"And get along home where we could soon be needed," Jesse added. "Still, we're the bunch of us alive."

"And that's the best kind of success," Willie agreed. "Home, then?"

"Home," the others cried.

CHAPTER 17

The others told and retold the story of the Shanklin place raid, finding something new to cheer each time. Willie only brooded and waited for the inevitable retaliation. It wasn't long in coming. Less than a week passed before a pair of riders splashed down the river, firing off their pistols and scaring the younger Slocum boys half to death. Lamar managed to drive off the attackers with a pair of well-placed rifle shots, but Willie knew it was but a temporary setback.

"That was just Fairchild's way of letting us know he's still out there," Willie explained. "Next time the bullets'll be fired at people, not in the air."

As a result both ranches took new precautions. No one rode alone. Whenever supply wagons visited Albany or Weatherford, they were escorted by a half-dozen riders. The children were kept close by, and visits from friends and neighbors were discouraged.

"I miss Tim's rides," Mike Cobb said over a dinner of pork chops and candied yams. "I never get any news from town now."

"Wasn't safe," Travis said. "You wouldn't want your friends hurt."

"No, sir," Mike agreed. But Willie could tell the isolation grated on the boy.

In the week that followed, neither the Cobbs nor the Slocums were much bothered by Fairchild's riders. True, two or three horsemen would appear on the fringes of the range. Often they would hurl insults or encourage pursuit. Willie recognized such tactics, and he warned the cowboys to hold their ground and give the other side a wide berth.

Then, with the first chill breezes of October whining through the baring trees, Fairchild sent a band of raiders onto the TS to bring death and destruction. A pair of cowboys intercepted the raid and blunted its impact, but they paid a high price. One lay dead and a second was badly wounded.

Lewis appeared with the news.

"Pa said you and Mr. Cobb'd want to have a look at how they did it," Lewis told Willie. "I know the place. I could take you there."

"I'll be half the day at my labors," Travis explained. "Can it wait for tomorrow?"

"Skies look full o' rain," Lewis explained. "Might wash out the tracks."

"I'll go," Willie said, motioning for Travis to continue with his work. "If Jesse finishes chasing that bunch of cattle up Yule Creek, send him along. Wouldn't hurt to have an extra gun."

"It's a promise," Travis answered. "Keep a weather eye out for trouble. Fairchild's about due to try somethin'."

Overdue by my thinking, Willie told himself. He didn't share those doubts with Lewis, though.

The two of them rode close to four miles along the river before Lewis located a pair of twinned hills where the river formed a broad bend. Cattle grazed on the rich grass beside the river, but the high ground above was a tangle of cactus, briers, scrub oak, and junipers.

Perfect place for an ambush," Willie noted. "This where it happened?"

"Yeah, right over there," Lewis said, pointing to an oval-shaped pile of rocks marking the grave of the unfortunate cowboy.

Willie waved his hat at the nearby longhorns, clearing a path. Lewis rode past, waving Willie along toward the hillside. To his left a half-dozen rocks suddenly cascaded down the slope, and Willie froze.

"Lewis, get around on my right!" Willie shouted as he drew a pistol.

"It's just me, General," Gil Cooksey called, stepping out onto a protruding boulder. "I been watchin' the stock."

"By yourself?" Willie asked.

"Was another fellow, but he, uh, rode off, uh, to fetch us some food," the boy explained. "Kind o' glad to see familiar faces."

"I expect so," Willie confessed. "Lewis, I didn't think your papa had anyone out this way not partnered up."

"Shouldn't," Lewis declared. "Most likely that cowboy got hungry and set off to bring some food up himself. Pa would've sent it by."

Willie nodded and turned back toward Gil. The boy appeared oddly pale, and he seemed to be shivering. His clothes were little more than tatters, of course, but Willie hadn't noticed that hard-nosed youngster showing signs of fright before. Not even in the Flat . . .

"Where's your horse got to, Gil?" Willie suddenly asked.

"Got him tied up, uh, over yonder a bit."

There was something in Gil's eye that warned otherwise. And Willie saw a shadow. . . .

"Lew, ride!" Willie shouted as he flattened himself against Stinger's neck and charged the hill. "Ride!"

Lewis instantly spurred his horse into a gallop, but a pair of rifle shots whizzed past where the young man rode. He cried out, then slumped to one side as his brown stallion carried him along toward safety.

"Jump on, Gil!" Willie urged as he pulled alongside the youngster. Gil's hands were bound, though, and a familiar face grinned from behind the boy's shoulder.

"He's kind o' occupied presently," white-haired Caswell Jarett said, waving a rifle at Willie's belly.

"Remember us?" Caswell's brother Jerome asked, appearing ten feet away with another rifle, and three cowboys completed the encirclement.

"I remember," Willie muttered. "Should've shot better back at the Flat."

"Sorry, Willie," Gil said as rough hands reached out and tore Willie from his horse. "I was partnered up with Mitch Lofland over there. Didn't know he was makin' Fairchild money."

"It's an easy enough mistake to make," Willie muttered as Cas and Jerome bound his hands behind his back. "Hard to recognize all the snakes by their bands sometimes."

"So, did we surprise you?" Romney Fairchild asked as he joined the small gathering. "I have been meaning to repay your attentions."

"Have you?" Willie asked, staring coldly at Fairchild. "Well, nothing's stopping you."

"No, it isn't," Fairchild said, driving a fist into Willie's middle. Willie convulsed in pain and dropped to his knees. "There, you *are* human. I always thought so. Now, I think I'll turn the entertainment over to these two fine young men. Friends of yours, I understand."

"Not friends," Willie said, spitting at Cas Jarrett's cackling face.

Cas responded by slamming an elbow across Willie's nose. The pain was sharp and sudden this time, but Willie didn't stagger. A second blow, and a third, set his ears to ringing. He could feel blood running down his nose.

"Stop it!" Gil yelled. "You swore you wouldn't hurt him. All you wanted was to talk to him. Remember?"

"I'd be a mute if I were you!" Fairchild advised Gil. "It's only Christian charity that's saved your life. No great imagination's necessary to determine how the major here found his way into our camp unseen."

"Want us to work on him, too?" Jerome Jarrett asked. "No extra charge, Mr. Fairchild."

Willie dipped his head and flung himself at Jerome. The suddenness of the movement caught the villain by surprise, and Willie managed to butt Jerome hard, then block him against a knotted oak.

"Ugh!" Jerome grunted. He then collapsed in a heap, moaning and fighting for breath. His brother Caswell threw

Gil aside and leaped onto Willie's back, knocking him to the ground. The two wrestled for a moment. Willie managed to shake loose of his bonds and lay a pair of well-aimed fists onto Cas's forehead before two cowboys dragged him away.

"Hold him there just a minute," Cas said, angrily glaring at Willie's bloody face. "You'll pay now, Mr. Gray Hat." Jerome tossed his brother a knife, and Cas pressed the blade against Willie's throat.

"Open him up like an old hog, Cas!" Jerome urged. "Pay him back for my hand!"

Jerome peeled a black glove from his right hand and held up the scarred and mutilated flesh for all to see. The middle and ring fingers were mere stubs.

"Tell you what, Jerome," Caswell said, turning to his brother. "Maybe you'd like to do the cuttin'. Start with the hands, maybe. Or the ears. Mr. Fairchild's partial to cuttin' ears, I hear. Then we go ahead and work our way down till this fellow's nothin' but a lump. Well?"

"I'd take a turn," Jerome agreed, stepping over and taking the knife.

"No!" Gil screamed, racing over, hands bound and all, but Fairchild lifted his foot, and the boy went sprawling.

"Little later we'll have a go at you, boy," Jerome warned as he kicked Gil hard in the ribs. "Now, what'll we cut first?"

"Boys, while I truly would enjoy the sport," Fairchild interrupted, "I wonder if we might not speak a moment with the major first."

"Certainly, sir," Jerome said, pausing. "What would you like answered? Just you ask. It'll get it answered, I figure."

"Actually, I thought we might start with names," Fairchild said. "Yours, for example. Wil? Expect there's more to it than that. I've heard whispers, but as to the truth . . ."

"I've got about as many names as you do, Fairchild," Willie answered, spitting blood from his mouth. "You like to borrow yours off tombstones. Me, I make mine up as I go."

"He was a reb for sure, Mr. Fairchild," Cas said. "I seen

that old gray hat he had on, and folks say it's how he come to know Slocum and Cobb the both of 'em.''

"And what might you know, Gilbert?" Fairchild asked, turning to the boy. "You rode from town together, Cas says. Perhaps you exchanged tales.''

"I'll tell you nothin','' Gil muttered. "He was middlin' good to me, and I went and let this happen!''

"You'll do as you're told,'' Cas barked, kicking Gil again. The boy curled up in a ball, and Willie's eyes darkened.

"No need trouble the boy, Mr. Fairchild,'' Jerome said, grinning. "Major here's goin' to tell you. He don't like us amusin' ourselves with yon stableboy. Got a tender spot for children, this one. Always takin' up their cases, even the little black ones. You'd think a body'd find enough trouble o' his own without takin' on extra.''

Jerome then drew out a whip and cracked it in the air. The next stroke took most of Gil's shirt and a bit of flesh as well.

"Don't tell 'em nothin'!'' Gil screamed as he fought to crawl away. Fairchild blocked the retreat with the hard toe of his boot.

"That's enough!'' Willie growled as he fought to free himself. "You two feeling brave, are you? Let go my hands and we'll see how brave you really are.''

"Even up the odds?'' Cas asked, laughing. "No, got no call to make it easy on you. Now, what's your name?''

"It's Death!'' a new voice shouted from the other hill. He fired three rifle shots, and the cowboy holding Willie's right arm fell in a heap. Willie slung the other man at Jerome Jarrett.

"Lord A'mighty!'' the cowboy screamed as he fell upon the jagged blade of the younger Jarrett's knife.

Willie drew a pistol and fired at Fairchild, but the Englishman had already reached the safety of the knotted oak. Rifle shots had driven the surviving cowboy down the ridge, and Willie found only the Jarrett brothers remained in view.

"I'd be careful, Major,'' Cas warned as he shielded himself with Gil Cooksey's trembling frame.

"Gil?'' Willie asked as he tried to steady his hand and end the Jarretts' worthless lives.

"Go ahead and shoot!" Gil pleaded. "He's goin' to kill me anyhow!"

"You're right there, boy!" Jerome howled as he freed himself from the dead cowboy and slashed the stableboy with the drawn knife. Willie pressed his trigger, but the pistol misfired.

"Let's get, Cas!" Jerome urged, and the killers escaped. Willie stared at their departing shadows, his insides burning with anger.

"Be another day!" Cas warned from the cover of the brush just ahead.

"Bank on it!" Willie answered. "You'll pay then! I swear it!"

Down below, Fairchild and his henchmen splashed into the river. The nearby rifleman threw five shots in that direction, but none of them found a target. Then, as the devils disappeared over the far ridge, a solitary figure stepped out of the shadows.

"Jess?" Willie cried in surprise.

"Expectin' General Robert E. Lee?" Jesse Cobb asked. "How's the boy?"

Willie only now knelt beside the writhing bundle that had been Gilbert Cooksey. The youngsters left arm was cut to the bone, and blood was everywhere.

"Bad!" Willie called to Jesse. "I need some bandages."

Gil's eyes barely seemed to follow his rescuer's movements. Willie tore his own shirt and that of the slain cowboy into strips and began binding the arm. The blood flow continued, and Willie reluctantly applied a tourniquet.

"Looks like you'll lose the arm," Willie said sourly. "Sorry, Gil, but I don't know anything to do."

"Ain't the arm . . . that's . . . the trouble," Gil managed to murmur. "Here."

Gil turned slightly, and Willie saw that the knife hadn't stopped at the arm. The blade had sliced into young Gil's side until it rested in the crook of his right thigh.

"Good Lord," Jesse cried as he gazed at the boy's side.

"What'd he say about openin' up a body like a butcher-shop hog?" Gil asked. "Did it fair, didn't he?"

145

Willie breathed deeply, then carefully withdrew the knife. He took a fresh armful of cloth strips and started binding the thigh and side. Gil hardly whimpered the whole time. But his eyes were growing faint, and the fingers of his good left hand clutched at Willie's arms.

"Did too good a job of it," Gil sobbed. "Lord, it hurts. Got me deep, he did."

"You're young," Willie said, fighting to steady his nerves. "I've seen men heal up with worse."

"You're a bad liar," the boy declared. "Thanks, Major."

Gilbert Cooksey then closed his eyes and rested his head on Willie's knee. He lay quietly for half an hour until Jesse tapped Willie's shoulder.

"He's gone and died," Jesse explained.

"I know," Willie confessed. "I felt him go. He wasn't much, you know, just a barn rat set upon by the worst kind of bad luck. He didn't deserve to be whipped, though, nor butchered, either."

"He didn't look so little atop a horse," Jesse said, bending over and taking the boy in his arms. "I don't suppose he'd take it bad if we put him with Pa and Bobby down by the river."

"I think he'd like that," Willie answered. "A boy who passed too many of his days alone oughtn't to be buried that way."

"When are we goin' after the others Willie?"

"When we're certain we can put an end to it," Willie responded. "After we bury Gil. Soon. Real soon, Jess."

CHAPTER 18

They did, indeed, set Gilbert Cooksey on the hill next to Bobby Cobb. Travis read from a Bible, and the little gathering shared a pair of hymns.

"Never gets easier, does it, Willie?" Travis asked as Willie shoveled dirt over Gil's blanket-covered corpse.

"We've had us some practice at it, I'll admit," Willie replied. "But it's not a job that endears itself to a man."

The two of them stood together a moment, staring into the distance and silently sharing memories of other times and places. Then Willie resumed his work, and Travis returned to his family.

Willie spent two days alternately mourning and riding the range searching for the Jarrett brothers. The killers failed to appear, but he spotted horsemen shadowing his movements.

"Got an urge to get shot?" he called to one pair. "Come down and have a closer look, won't you?"

The Cobb brothers and Ted Slocum mentioned the same sort of thing when Willie gathered everyone together for a war council.

"I can't stand this waitin'," Jesse Cobb spoke finally. "It's doin' us no good. They grow stronger, and we just lose sleep."

"He's right," Ted Slocum agreed. "I've got a boy hurt

back home. I don't plan to have another. We have to carry the fight to them.''

"But who's them?" Willie asked. "Fairchild? He's more like a Red River cardsharp than a cattle baron. And what's his weak link? We have to find it, friends."

It was that thought that sent Willie riding to Albany in the depths of a moonless night. He skirted the campfires of Fairchild riders and avoided the well-watched roads. Instead he made his way cross-country to the edge of town. It was near midnight when he rapped on the door of the Little house.

"What is it?" Grandpa Little called. "Don't you know it's the middle of the night?" The old man cursed and grumbled his way to the door. He grew quiet when he saw Willie's face through the window.

"I know it's late, sir," Willie admitted when Little opened the door, "but I've got a problem I can't get solved on my own."

"And you figure I've got your answers?" the clerk asked. "Ain't likely, son."

"Mr. Little, I've been north and west of here ten years, and I was off in the army the four or five before that. You know that well enough. I've got no friends in high places, nobody to send wires to banks or check records in Austin."

"And you guess I do?" the old man asked. "Son, I'm just a worn-out old shoe. People give me papers to stick here and there. They put a few pennies in my pocket to keep up the jailhouse."

"Grandpa, help him," Tim urged as he stepped to the door beside his grandfather. "You always talk about the old days when people pitched in and helped each other, when the law meant more'n a star on somebody's shirt. That Fairchild fellow shot Bobby Cobb. They fired bullets at *me*! I knew Gil Cooksey, too, Major. He was a good boy 'fore his pa died. If I hadn't had Grandpa, I might've ended up the same."

"I wouldn't have you run any risks, sir," Willie added. "I don't plan to run any myself. It's just, well, I've got a brother who's done well."

148

"Don't I know that?" Little asked. "It's hard not to live along the Brazos River and not know Sam Delamer!"

"I meant another brother," Willie said with dark, brooding eyes. "He's in Austin now, to hear folks tell it. In government. I think maybe a state senator'd have the kind of information I need."

"And?"

"If I send a telegram to him direct, I got a feeling word might just get to Fairchild. He seems to have eyes and ears everywhere."

"He pays the clerk at the telegraph office and the stage drivers both," Tim explained. "Sometimes wires never get sent."

"I suspected as much," Willie muttered.

"What you need's to get a man to Austin," Little declared. "With the questions you need answered."

"That's it exactly," Willie explained.

"They'd take notice of anybody leavin' Albany."

"Unless it was someone with an official reason," Willie pointed out. "Surely you must make a swing to the capital now and again."

"At tax-collectin' time," Little admitted. "Right about now."

"I've written out what I need, sir," Willie said, passing over a thick envelope. "It's to go to Mr. James F. Delamer. Get it to him personally, if you please. I'd as soon my other brother not know I'm about."

"Understand why," the clerk said, nodding. "I do this, you'll have to look after Tim."

"I don't suppose he'd mind a few days at the Cobb place?" Willie asked.

"No, sir!" Tim cried. "Ain't seen Mike in a bit."

"Then it's settled," Grandpa Little declared. "I'll give it two days' pause. Then I'll head south. Best you take Tim the same mornin' I leave. He goes before, and somebody'll sniff up a skunk."

"Watch yourself, sir," Willie warned. "And you, Tim. Not a hint to anybody."

"Not a hint," Tim agreed.

149

Willie then shook hands with them both and turned toward Stinger. Moments later he was back in the shadows, a ghost carried upon the silent wind.

The two days seemed to take forever, and the week that followed was an additional trial. November arrived with its cold nights and rainy days. Twice the range was shrouded in heavy fog. Each time the Jarretts raided stock and shot at cowhands. No one was killed, but three TS cowboys were hurt. A pair of Fairchild hirelings were hit as well.

"Don't you suppose Grandpa ought to be back by now?" Tim asked when his patience, too, began to fail.

"Ted Slocum sends a pair of riders to Albany every night to check," Willie explained. "So far there's been no word. Of course, your grandpa wouldn't be one to send a wire or write a letter. He wouldn't want Fairchild informed of our plans. No, he'll come back on the stage and send word for us to come to town to get the news."

"Sure," the boy mumbled.

As it happened, Grandpa Little didn't return on the stage, though. Instead a carriage rumbled up to the Cobb house.

"What the devil's this?" Travis demanded to know, waving a shotgun at the driver.

"It's just me," Little announced as he climbed out of the coach. "And a friend."

A slender dark-haired young man in his early twenties stepped out as well. His winning smile and fine tailored suit marked him as something of a curiosity on the Texas frontier.

"Just ain't possible," Jesse cried, staring at the apparition before him.

"It's been a while, Jess," the stranger answered. "Am I so changed, Trav?"

"Don't you fellows recognize your own state senator?" Little asked. "James Fannin Delamer!"

Willie had heard most of it and seen some, but the announcement of his brother's name struck at him like a sharp dart of thunder. Willie's knees buckled, and he wanted to hide. Was it possible this tall, handsome young man was the little brother who used to huddle at his side on winter nights?

Was this the Jamie who pleaded for stories or begged a ride to the river? It couldn't be!

"I think we've got a surprise for you, too," Travis said, whispering for Jesse to fetch Willie. "You're not the first unexpected guest to visit Shackleford County this year."

"I know," Jamie said, searching the other faces. "Where is he?"

Willie reluctantly emerged from the barn. Jesse pulled him along until the two Delamers stared upon each other. Eyes grew moist. Wrists clasped each other, and then Willie pulled his brother close.

"Jamie, you've gone and grown into the best manner of man," Willie observed. "Read the law, I heard, and now turned to government."

"And what've you become since driving those steers to Kansas?"

"The worst kind of a fool," Willie confessed. "Near killed a dozen times, and scarred up worse'n a Galveston tattoo shop."

"All that's over," Jamie announced as he led Willie aside. "You're home."

"Not home," Willie argued as they strolled down to the river. "I can never go home, either."

"What?"

"Don't you know why I didn't come back from Kansas?" Willie asked. "Sam hired me dead."

"Doesn't surprise me," Jamie said, scowling. "He packed me off to read the law, then got me elected to office so I'd be out of the way. I keep an eye on the books, just the same. And I've got a bigger slice of the business than he'd care to know."

"See to it he doesn't," Willie warned. "You never had the eye with a rifle I did."

"No," Jamie confessed. "But I've learned a few other tricks. And made powerful friends."

"Then you were able to find out about this Fairchild fellow."

"Not everything. But enough."

Jamie then drew out a notebook and began the strange tale

of how a New Orleans gambler could become the scourge of Shackleford County.

"In the beginning," Jamie explained, "he only purchased land for others. Was the agent of the sale, you see. Later he became a full partner. The thing is, though, his financing is all British, and the men there prefer to keep a low profile. They would never agree to what's been going on lately. I know. I sent word to London.

"You'll like the second part not a bit. The financing's come from two banks. One in Jacksboro and the other in Austin. Both times the loans were secured by one Sam H. Delamer. Familiar name, eh?"

"I smelled it all along."

"The holdings Sam pledged to guarantee those loans aren't his alone, Willie. I filed court injunctions before leaving. The banks will soon be calling those notes, and unless Fairchild's got money set aside, he's finished. What's even better, I doubt he'll be able to pay taxes on the land he holds now. That means the county will take possession of every last acre. Ted Slocum, who's got the resources to do it, could buy up that strip west of his place for ten cents on the dollar. Maybe less."

"All this's is moving pretty fast. Best we slow it a hair. I'll have Grandpa Little wait a week to send the tax notices. That way they won't tie him into things. That wouldn't be altogether healthy."

"No, nor would it be for me to stay long. I'll leave come dark."

"Jamie, I wish it didn't have to be that way," Willie said, gripping his brother's shoulders. "My head's so full of stories and memories, and I feel as if I'm coming back to life."

"You are, in a way," Jamie observed. "I was told you died."

"It was for the best."

"No, it wasn't," Jamie mumbled bitterly. "It left me more alone than you'll ever know. Mama and Papa were gone. Mary too. All I had was Sam, and there's not a soft spot to him! Between the two of us we might have fought him, kept

152

the ranch as Papa wanted it. Instead you gave up, and I, well, I survived.''

''You were young, Jamie, and you hadn't just fought yourself a war. The Civil War, people are starting to call it. War Between Brothers. Well, that's the same sort of fight Sam and I'd have had. I hear young Robert's coming to be a fine boy.''

''He's my clerk in Austin.''

''Would he have much use for either of us had we killed his father?''

''It wouldn't have come to that.''

''Yes, it would have,'' Willie insisted. ''You put two bucks head-to-head, one'll drive the other away. Put two men up, and one'll kill the other.''

''And is that how it will be with Romney Fairchild?'' Jamie asked.

''Put yourself in Trav's shoes. That Englishman killed his brother,'' Willie pointed out. ''What sympathy's to be found for him?''

Jamie nodded. The two Delamers then examined the sketches and maps Jamie had brought from Austin. In short order Willie understood them each and every one. He also viewed with smug satisfaction Fairchild's overextended banking accounts. A man with a fortune in mortgaged land stood a poor chance when the banks began calling in notes.

''I know you're bound and determined to finish here,'' Jamie said in conclusion. ''It's good country for cattle, so maybe you'll grab a share of the range yourself. It would please me to think I had a part in making that happen. Meanwhile, why not visit Austin before you make any plans? You'd find the place changed. Good luck, Willie. I'd tell you to be careful, but you wouldn't do it. You couldn't have changed that much.''

The brothers shared a laugh. Then Willie escorted Jamie to the coach, and the vehicle turned and headed off southward.

''I'll escort you back to Albany after dark,'' Willie promised the Littles. ''First, though, we've got a couple of things to plan out.''

CHAPTER 19

In the days that followed, Willie watched with no small satisfaction as events tightened Romney Fairchild's coffin screws. It wasn't long before the Englishman discovered his funds drying up, and Fairchild's frequent telegrams to Jacksboro and Austin were a sure sign of desperation. Then, when Sheriff Pennypacker presented the county's annual tax bill, Fairchild became hysterical.

"How am I to pay such a sum overnight?" he screamed. "I need time."

"Oh, you have a while," the sheriff advised. "Some folks take a week. I've known the county to wait a whole month After that we generally look into holdin' auctions."

"Really, Sheriff, you can't imagine I won't settle accounts given time."

"For all I know you'd use that extra time to drive your stock off, maybe sell to some fellow who didn't know taxes were owed on the property. Wire your banker friends for the money. It's sure to get here in a month."

Tim Little, who heard the conversation and passed it along to Willie, described Fairchild's face as mottled purple. Willie imagined it so. A man with his fingers on future prosperity is apt to fret when it slips from his grasp.

Fairchild nevertheless kept up appearances. He continued to make offers for land, and he kept his men riding the fringes

154

of the Cobb and Slocum ranches. Fewer and fewer riders watched the roads, though, and the more experienced cowboys began to leave.

"I talked to a couple o' them boys yesterday," Jesse declared. "Offered to come over to our side if we'd feed 'em through winter. Ain't a one of 'em been paid for a month now, save them Jarretts, and it rankles the good ones. This fight's about won, I'd judge."

Willie knew otherwise. It was when a man relaxed his guard that the enemy always struck. So he urged Travis and Ted Slocum to keep lookouts posted by night and pair up the cowboys riding the range. And when Elvira and Elyssia Slocum agreed with Irene Cobb that a trip to Albany was in order, Willie insisted on escorting them personally.

"That's a trip I could miss real easy," Mike announced.

"Give you a chance to visit Tim," Willie pointed out.

"I'll do that once the war's over," Mike said, grinning. " 'Sides, I'm bound to watch Josh and Art while Ma's away."

Travis and Jesse did go, together with Lamar and Lewis Slocum. Every one of them carried a rifle, and there wasn't an instant when several wary eyes weren't scanning every inch of the surrounding countryside.

As it happened, the trip to Albany was uneventful. Willie didn't even spy the usual shadowing riders. Once in town, the women set about filling their lists at the mercantile. Willie picked up a few boxes of shells and visited with Grandpa Little.

"Can't be long now," the old man explained. "The Jacksboro bank sent a man to town with a claim on the Shanklin place. I expect to file on the land for the county in another few weeks. Every day Nate Pennypacker runs a few more stray Fairchild hands out of town. No, it can't be much longer."

Willie had his own opportunity to view Romney Fairchild later that afternoon. The Englishman stood outside the telegraph office staring at a handful of wires.

"Bad news?" Willie called.

"Let me, Boss," Jerome Jarrett begged, fingering the rifle at his side.

"What'd you say, Gray Hat?" Cas asked. "Callin' me out, was you?"

"No, I was just asking how Mr. Fairchild's business was doing," Willie explained. "Some hands rode by the other day saying they hadn't been paid in weeks, and that you were losing your land because of unpaid taxes."

"That's a lie!" Cas answered, gazing nervously at his employer. "Tell him, Mr. Fairchild."

"I expect any moment to hear encouraging news from my bankers," Fairchild responded. "They should have my money here momentarily."

"What money's that?" Willie asked. "The two thousand you owe in Jacksboro or the twenty-five you owe in Austin?"

"You couldn't know," Fairchild said, stunned.

"I have friends, too," Willie asserted.

"No," Fairchild muttered. "You couldn't have that long a reach."

"No, but somebody does. He might be a fellow lives downriver and deemed you had a little bit too much land here for to be a comfortable neighbor."

"Oh?" Fairchild asked. "Who might that be?"

"Oh, we needn't mention names," Willie said, grinning as the words ate at Fairchild. "His steers wear a fork on their rump, though. Trident, that is."

"The scoundrel!" Fairchild shouted. "He said he wanted Cobb and Slocum cleared from the river. He even mentioned me to his bankers. Ah, a fine trap I fell into."

"Now it's over," Willie declared. "Wise man'd head out while he's still got hide and horns."

"It would seem I have little choice," Fairchild grumbled. "No choice, in point of fact."

"You're too slippery to leave a back way out," Willie explained. "I hear there's good country out in New Mexico Territory. Long ways from here. You might enjoy the climate."

"Might," Fairchild declared. The Englishman's face betrayed a mixture of disappointment and rage. Willie warned himself not to abandon the cautious path quite yet.

Others had already done so. Willie was helping load boxes

of supplies into the open beds of two wagons when Mike Cobb rode his lathered pony into Albany.

"Pa!" the boy shouted. "Ma! They took 'em!"

"Took who?" Travis demanded as he trotted to his boy's side. "Calm down and spell it out."

"He needn't," Romney Fairchild said, stepping out into the street with the Jarretts. "It's a simple matter actually. You men have created no small difficulty for me. I, therefore, choose to do the same for you."

"Look familiar?" Jerome Jarrett asked, holding up a small calico shirt. Cas held a second garment to the light, and Irene identified them.

"Trav, Art and Josh were wearing those shirts when we left home," she answered.

"Riders came," Mike explained. "The three of us were down at the river. I managed to get to my horse and get away. One man took Art, and another one grabbed Josh."

"You'll bleed for this," Willie declared, stepping into the street opposite the kidnappers.

"No, Willie," Travis pleaded. "The boys—"

"Are in other hands," Willie declared. "We'll go get 'em soon enough. Fairchild here'll take us there once his friends are dead."

"Hold up there!" Sheriff Pennypacker yelled as he stepped between the warring groups. "You'll not fight your war in my town. Off with you all and leave Albany to its peace."

"They've taken my boys, Sheriff!" Irene screamed. "Do something!"

"What proof—" the sheriff began.

"They have Art's shirt. Josh's too," Irene insisted.

"Oh, they might've stumbled across those shirts any-place," Pennypacker answered. "If the boys don't turn up in a few days, let me know. I'll have a look 'round."

"Are you that blind?" Travis asked.

"My eyes are good enough to see who I might have to lock up in my jailhouse," the sheriff replied. "Now get along home, folks. Take your trouble elsewhere! Otherwise I'll be usin' my shotgun."

"What about justice?" Irene called.

"It's taken a week or two off," Cas replied. "As for your boys, lady, we'll find 'em for you. Be nice to get a reward. What did you say you'd pay? Two thousand dollars? That'd do. Have the gray-hat fellow bring the money at dawn."

"Where?" Irene asked.

"The river, down where it bends past the old Shanklin place," Jerome answered. "They call it Turkey Hollow. Dawn. We'll be waitin'."

"Sure, they will," Jesse objected. "In ambush. No, let's make it elsewhere."

"You won't make it anywhere!" Fairchild shouted. "Major, bring the money to the hollow at sunrise. If you don't, I'll have some ears to send you. They're a good deal easier to bury than a whole corpse, you know. Unless the vultures have a go at the body first."

Irene cursed the Englishman. Travis had to restrain Jesse from firing at the villains. Willie merely nodded his understanding. The Jarretts escorted Fairchild out of town, and Willie finished loading the supply wagons.

"You can't go, of course," Travis declared when they started back to the ranch. "They're certain to have an ambush planned."

"Would be likely, Trav," Willie agreed. "Only he wasn't kidding about those ears. If I don't think out a better way to get those boys clear, I'll go."

"Willie . . ."

"You'd do it yourself, Trav. I know it. Whatever else happens, I want your sons to grow tall on the Brazos. We've buried enough boys hereabouts, the two of us."

"I should go with you," Travis added.

"No, it's for me to do alone. It's what I'm best at."

CHAPTER 20

Willie didn't sleep well that night. A parade of phantoms haunted his dreams, and it was a relief when he rolled off his bunk in the predawn darkness inside the barn and shook himself awake.

"Isn't the first time," he muttered as he exchanged his nightshirt for dark woolen shirt and trousers. Dark clothes were best for the task ahead. He next pulled on his boots. Finally he fished out the old gray hat and set it at his side as he broke down his twin pistols and began the chore of cleaning. He'd tended to the Winchester the night before.

It was still dark when Willie emerged from the barn and headed for the corral. Stinger stirred anxiously at the sight of Willie, saddle draped over one shoulder, emerging in the dim light.

"Ain't you gettin' ahead o' yourself a hair, Willie?" Travis Cobb called.

Willie studied the corral rail a moment. At last he detected two shadowy shapes there—Travis and Jesse Cobb.

"I told you before," Willie said, shuddering from a sudden November chill. "It's a job to be done alone."

"Ain't either," Jesse protested. "To begin with, you don't know that hollow. Then there's the boys to consider. Even if you was to keep them Jarretts occupied, you'd never get Josh and Art clear o' Fairchild unharmed."

"He's right," Travis agreed. "You go alone, all you'll get accomplished is yourself dead. Won't help us a bit."

"I got a different plan," Jesse explained. "First off, I got word to Ted Slocum. He'll have some men on the river east and west to watch who comes. There already, I'd guess. Trav and I'll slide around to the north and come down through the gullies, cross the river, and get in back of 'em. They'll be on the east side, leavin' you to face the sun, wouldn't you think? Nasty stretch o' ground that, with rocks and washes all over the place. Like I said yesterday, it's a perfect spot for an ambush. Or even two of 'em."

"So I'm the bait to draw the rats," Willie observed. "I'll go along with it providing you swear you'll get the little ones clear before joining in with the shooting. That clear enough, Trav?"

"I don't see you've got a choice in this, Willie. And I don't like the notion of you tradin' bullets with a handful o' bushwhackers. That fool luck o' yours can't last forever."

"Won't be luck gets this job done," Willie told them. "Be coldhearted shooting and pure anger!"

"Willie . . ." Travis started to argue, but Willie was already saddling Stinger. He turned and nodded his agreement to the plan and motioned his friends to ride out. Willie followed ten minutes later.

He had only the vaguest notion as to where Turkey Hollow might be, but he remembered the Shanklin place just fine. As he rode past the charred remains of the ranch, he heard the echoes of gunfire and screaming roll through his memory. He could smell an odor of death on the place. Unburied bodies remained in the rubble—eerie white bones picked clean by the buzzards.

Willie found himself seeing faces. There was grinning Bobby Cobb and little Gil Cooksey. Those faces kindled a raging inferno in Willie's soul, and he swore to them the man who had brought their deaths would this morning take his final steps upon the earth.

"You're dead, Fairchild," Willie vowed. The old hardness had come to him. No shudder of hesitation set his fingers to trembling. No, he was ready.

So was Fairchild. He stood near a line of boulders, one hand gripping the slender neck of Art Cobb and the other upon little brother Josh. A bit farther back three cowboys stood watch over the river. The Jarretts huddled in the rocks on either side of their boss.

"Well, I'll be!" Cas Jarrett cried when Willie rode closer in the faint light creeping over the hills to the east. "I never thought you'd be such a fool to come alone."

"I brought the money," Willie called, tossing a leather pouch filled with rags onto the sandy ground between himself and Fairchild. "Now let the youngsters go!"

"Later," Fairchild said, waving for one of the cowboys to fetch the pouch. Willie flashed an angry eye at the young drover, and the cowboy dove to cover.

"First the boys," Willie insisted.

"Gordon, King, come take these boys," Fairchild yelled. "I'll get the money myself."

"Don't do it!" Jerome Jarrett warned. "This ain't about money, and we all know it. He wouldn't bring you anything but grief, Boss."

"Worried you won't get paid?" Willie asked.

"Oh, we'll be rewarded for this day's labors," Cas argued. "Your hide'd be payment enough for that, eh, Jerome?"

Jerome gazed at his mutilated hand and glared.

"Take the boys," Fairchild ordered, and two of the cowboys threaded their way to the Englishman and took charge of the children. They started back toward the river, but they never got there. Two rifle shots punctuated the frosty air, and the cowboys dropped like flour sacks off the back of a supply wagon. Travis rushed over and pulled his boys to safety while Jesse blasted the third cowboy.

"Now, that evens it all up, doesn't it?" Willie called as he rolled off Stinger's side and raced to the cover of a nearby boulder. Bullets peppered the sandy ground behind him, but none found a target.

"Cas, take the right!" Jerome yelled.

"No, come back!" Fairchild cried. "There are men behind me."

"That's your worry, Boss!" Jerome exclaimed. "We got business to tend."

So it was that Willie squared off with the Jarretts. He never doubted it would end up that way. His sole concern had been for the little ones, and now that they were safely in their father's care, nothing remained but a bit of hunting.

Like stalking turkeys, Willie thought. These had sharp teeth, though, and Willie took care to keep his own hide behind cover.

As with any hunt, the trick was knowing the game. And using every sense. Willie could practically smell those Jarretts, and his ears picked up heavy breathing nearby. With subtle movement Willie snaked his way through the rocks until he was around behind the left-hand man. The other, too, was closing in. A sudden notion struck Willie, and he couldn't help grinning. He crawled along ten feet or so until he had a clear view of Caswell Jarrett's back. Then he glimpsed Jerome.

Say your prayers, boys, Willie thought as he gripped a small stone and hurled it at Cas Jarrett's back. He then fired a shot toward a rock three feet behind Jerome's feet.

"Ahh!" Cas cried, instinctively leaping to his feet. Jerome, startled by the near miss and stung by splinters of rock, opened up on the first hint of movement. Five bullets sprayed the hollow, and three of them exploded through Cas Jarrett's chest.

"Jerome?" the elder killer cried, his eyes crying betrayal even as they clouded with death.

"Cas!" Jerome screamed as his brother fell.

Now it's your turn, Willie thought as he fixed the younger man in his slights. Jerome had lost all hint of sense and was rushing across open ground, firing the empty chambers of his pistol as he shouted to his dead brother. Willie paused a moment, for it was a hard thing to shoot down a madman. But the image of Gil Cooksey's butchered side flooded Willie's mind. No, you've killed for the last time! Willie thought, aiming and firing a single bullet through Jerome's forehead. The young killer spun around and fell dead on the spot.

"Jerome? Cas?" Fairchild screamed.

"They've finished their business," Willie called. The words echoed across the hollow, and Fairchild scrambled toward a line of waiting horses. Jesse Cobb appeared before him, though, scattering the horses and chasing Fairchild back into the hollow. The Englishman tried to escape in the other direction, but Ted Slocum appeared.

"Look here!" Fairchild shouted, flinging aside a pistol. "I'm unarmed. You wouldn't shoot down a helpless man, would you?"

"Didn't stop you from shootin' my brother!" Jesse replied angrily.

"Nor little Gil Cooksey," Willie added. "You've set your bloody hands on boys that never offered you so much as a cross word, and you've threatened half this county with death—or worse."

"He's got a point, though, Willie," Travis argued. "I never shot an unarmed man."

"Nor me," Slocum added.

"Unarmed?" Willie asked. "He's done none of the shooting himself. His weapon's a stack of banknotes. His tool's any man with a pistol. Look around you at this place. Who's brought death here? Who's the real killer?"

"He'll have a trial," Travis argued. "And then hang."

"Will he?" Willie asked. "I've seen enough men slip their bonds to know better. He'll only blame the Jarretts, and somebody will look at his fine clothes and gentlemanly manners and judge he couldn't be capable of such cold-blooded business."

"So what do we do?" Travis asked.

"Settle it here and now," Willie told them. "If you've got no stomach for it, ride along. I'll deal with Mr. Romney Fairchild."

The Englishman turned to the others and grinned with all the charm of a cobra. "Gentlemen, you can't turn away from law," he pleaded. "It's what separates us from the wild animals."

"Nothing does that!" Willie barked. "Except maybe that they don't prey on their own kind."

"You can't mean to leave me here with this wild man?"

Fairchild shouted as Ted Slocum collected his men and set off. Travis ushered his boys toward waiting horses and got the little ones mounted. Only Willie and Jesse remained.

"Please!" Fairchild begged. "I can help you."

"Help yourself," Willie urged as he stared hard at the whimpering ruin of his enemy.

"Let me," Jesse said, pulling a pistol and stepping to Fairchild's side. "For Bobby."

"No!" Fairchild cried, throwing himself on the ground. Jesse hesitated, and the Englishman dug a pocket Colt from his boot and aimed it as Jesse's head. Willie instinctively fired, striking Fairchild just below the right eye and folding him up like a blanket. The pocket pistol discharged harmlessly in the air, and Jesse thereupon emptied his pistol into Fairchild's lifeless frame.

"Willie?" Jesse called.

"Never can trust a snake, Jess," Willie responded. "This one had a cardsharp's hands, remember? Always got to have a hold card up one sleeve. Or in a boot."

"Gettin' to be a habit, you savin' my hide."

"Not so bad a vice as some," Willie pointed out.

Travis reappeared, his pale face painted with worry, but Willie waved at his old friend, and Jesse greeted his brother with a grim smile.

"So, it's over, is it?" Travis asked.

"Yes," Willie agreed.

"Funny," Jesse said as he kicked Fairchild to make certain the villain wouldn't spring to life again. "I figured to feel better when it was all done."

"Too many graves dug to warm a man's heart," Willie observed. "But at least there aren't any more waiting to get filled."

CHAPTER 21

Ted Slocum had a pair of cowboys haul Fairchild and the Jarretts to Albany that next day. The three unfortunate cowboys were buried beside the river where they fell.

"There's a kinship of sorts among range hands," Slocum noted as he passed on the news to Willie and Travis.

"Sure," Willie agreed. "Was just bad circumstance led those three astray. What'd the sheriff say when he saw Fairchild?"

"Ordered a five-dollar county funeral," Slocum explained. "As for the Jarretts, he sent some wires. Seems they were wanted down on the Pecos. There's a hundred dollars' reward coming."

"That much?" Willie asked, shaking his head somberly. "It would have been a disappointment to the pair of 'em."

"I thought, if you didn't object, we might pass the money on to Miz Amanda Snodgrass in Weatherford," Slocum added.

"She's started up a home for orphans there," Jesse said, nodding his agreement. "Be sort of a memorial for Gil and Bobby."

"I'd favor that," Willie told them. "Might have a couple of hundred more to hand over."

"For that kind of money you could buy up a nice acreage here on the Clear Fork," Travis observed. "Shanklin place

165

goes up for sale next week. The rest of Fairchild's holdings are in the hands of the county. I don't expect them to bargain too hard a price."

"I'm not much for settling anywhere," Willie said, frowning. "Got itchy feet already."

"Not with winter comin' on," Travis objected. "That's a time to pass with family."

"He's right, Uncle Wil," Jesse added, slapping Willie's back.

"Already been here months," Willie explained. "Longer'n I intended."

"No time at all," Travis argued. "We've hardly gotten proper acquainted. Be a fine time to go after mule deer in the river thickets. And you haven't told the boys half the stories they'll want."

"Be better times now Fairchild's finished," Jesse declared. "Maybe time to race a horse or two. Or hunt up range ponies."

"Cold for swimmin', but there's comfort sittin' by a warm fire," Travis added. "Willie, you've been too long gone from this country. You belong here. I don't have to tell you that. You know it deep down, in your bones.

"I hoped you'd share a fine summer and find this a place of peace and rest."

"So did I," Willie said sadly.

"Well, that didn't work out," Travis admitted. "But there's a winter to sort through your feelin's and find that peace."

"I'm not sure there's peace to be found in this life," Willie told them. "I've looked for it high and low, but it never lasts more than a particle of a second. So it seems, anyway. I did find friends here, though, and a sort of belonging I never expected to feel again. All in all, it's not been such a bad bargain."

"Give us a chance to make it better yet," Travis urged.

"If you tire of these fellows, we've got room for you at the TS," Slocum added.

"We're short a man in the house now Bobby's gone," Jesse declared. "Time you came in from the barn."

"And off the range," Travis argued. "You said you came

here to find something. Isn't possible to have everything that was here before the war, Willie. Your folks are gone. Sam's got the ranch. But it seems to me Jamie went a bit out of the way to help out, and he'd likely welcome a visit in return. Meanwhile, stay here with those who'd have you. You're family. Don't you see that? This belongin' you talk about's a bond of sorts between you and all o' us. I never knew Willie Delamer to break his bond.''

Irene brought the children out then, and Davy happened over from the corral. With all the Cobbs there, reaching out and urging him to remain, the distant call of open country became mute.

''Winter's no time to ride alone,'' Travis said for what seemed the hundredth time.

''I guess not,'' Willie said, surrendering. ''I remember how I set off into the Rockies one time, though.''

The youngsters huddled close against the autumn chill, and Willie warmed at their touch. For once belonging had chased away the specter of death. Gazing into the bright faces and sincere eyes, Willie knew Travis had been right. It *was* time to come in off the range. ''Out of the wilderness,'' his father would have called it. Home!

ABOUT THE AUTHOR

G. Clifton Wisler comes by his interest in the West naturally. Born in Oklahoma and raised in Texas, he discovered early on a fascination for the history of the region. His first novel, MY BROTHER, THE WIND, received a nomination for the American Book Award in 1980. Among the many others that have followed are THUNDER ON THE TENNESSEE, winner of the Western Writers of America Spur Award for Best Western Juvenile Book of 1983; WINTER OF THE WOLF, a Spur finalist in 1982; and Delamer Westerns THE TRIDENT BRAND, STARR'S SHOWDOWN, PURGATORY, ABREGO CANYON, THE WAYWARD TRAIL, SWEETWATER FLATS, and SAM DELAMER. AMONG THE EAGLES, a Delamer Western, was honored by the Western Writers as best original paperback of 1989. In addition to his writing, Wisler frequently speaks to school groups and conducts writing clinics. He lives in Plano, Texas, where he is active in Boy Scouts.

G. CLIFTON WISLER

************ *presents* ************

THE DELAMER WESTERNS